ONE . . . TWO . . . THREE—DRAW!

Gathering all his strength Cam lunged for the man's gun, got it, lifted it out of the holster and then, hand on the bench, pushed himself to his feet. He brought the gun up, cocked, and now the crew, warned by a cry from a man across the table, came to their feet.

Cam backed off, the gun held before him, and the crew fell silent.

Finally one man across the table spoke, "If we all go for our guns at the same time, we'll get him. Go on three. One—"

Cam shot him in the leg and the man spun over the bench with a howl of pain and fell heavily to the floor.

"Go on. Draw," Cam taunted. "You're only dead once."

THREE
FOR THE
MONEY

Luke Short

A DELL BOOK

Published by
Dell Publishing
a division of
Bantam Doubleday Dell Publishing Group, Inc.
666 Fifth Avenue
New York, New York 10103

ISBN: 0-440-20844-0

Reprinted by arrangement with the author's estate

Printed in the United States of America

Published simultaneously in Canada

February 1991

10 9 8 7 6 5 4 3 2 1

RAD

1

On that Monday night, the heat of the Arizona day was gone, and a dozen people were gathered on El Cuervo's station platform. They watched the train pull past them and brake to a stop, its lone passenger car abutting the station platform. The brakeman came out of the caboose with a stepping stool, placed it below the passenger car steps, called "All aboard, folks," then walked down the platform, stepped off it, and halted by the door of the baggage car. Its doors opened, and, by the light of the lantern inside, a few curious passengers watched a team back a buckboard up to the open door. They could even make out the legend of the sign on the side of the buckboard which read "Consolidated Mining and Milling Company."

Two guards with rifles got down from the bed of the buckboard and stood on either side of the team. They allowed the brakeman to climb on to the buckboard and step into the baggage car. The driver of the buckboard went back to the bed and wrestled two small, but heavy, crates onto the floor of the baggage car. Afterward, the two guards moved up into the baggage car and the door was rolled shut.

Inside the lamplit coach, a young man dressed in a townsman suit, and a beautiful young woman, moved toward the front of the car and sat down, the woman next to the window. The young man put their single valise in the overhead rack. As he finished, and began to seat himself beside her, two roughly dressed men passed them and took the seat closest to the baggage car.

1

The train began to move as the girl took off her gloves, and the rings on her left hand glittered in the lamplight as she raised her hands to remove her hat.

The train was well clear of the town of El Cuervo when the brakeman came through the half-glass door to the front of the car. As he shrugged into his uniform jacket, a gun rammed in his belt was plainly visible. He took the tickets from the two men in the first seat, then collected from Dan Bowers the tickets for him and his auburn-haired wife, Christina.

As the brakeman moved down the aisle, collecting tickets, the passenger next to the aisle ahead of the Bowers took a shard of mirror from his shirt pocket. Holding it in his hand on the armrest, he held it so he could watch the progress of the brakeman in its reflection. When the brakeman finished his ticket taking, and moved through the open door at the back end of the car, the man on the aisle said to his companion, "Now."

The two men rose and went out past the half-glass door and closed it. Almost immediately, and above the clatter of the train's wheels, came a sound of three gunshots. Bowers looked at his wife, but neither spoke.

Now, above the train sounds, they could hear a man running. The brakeman passed them, his gun drawn.

Dan Bowers rose, then pulled a gun from the holster under his coat, and followed the brakeman who now had reached the half-glass door.

In the reflections from the glass, the brakeman saw a man coming up behind him with a drawn gun. He wrenched the door open, moved out onto the platform, and then noted the door to the baggage car was half open. Instead of moving toward it, however, he took a step to his left and raised his gun. Dan Bowers yanked the door open and was stepping through the doorway when the brakeman shot at him. Bowers slammed into the doorframe and then fell back into the car, his feet propping open the door.

The brakeman, gun still in hand, moved into the doorway just in time to see Christina Bowers lunge from her seat, run the few short steps to her husband and kneel beside him.

2

Avoiding the blood welling from the chest shot, Mrs. Bowers felt for a pulse in her husband's throat. She held her finger against it until she was sure, and then she raised her head to look at the brakeman with pure hatred in her green eyes.

She said bitterly, "You fool, he was only trying to help you." She collapsed in a faint and sprawled beside her dead husband.

The Consolidated Mine and Milling offices lay on the wide shelf cut into a bare and rocky mountain that looked down on the sprawling mining town of El Cuervo. As he approached the Consolidated on his dun gelding Cameron Holgate heard the assorted noises coming from the hoist shack and head frame beyond the office. Two big ore wagons waited while a third under the huge bin was being loaded with ore. Most of the mine's activities, he knew, were underground, and only a shift change could show the number of miners working here.

Dismounting at the tie rail, he tramped toward the office door, a tall man dressed in worn range clothes that sifted tiny streamers of dust at each movement. Halting before the door, he took off his stetson, and, with it, beat the dust from his shirt and trousers. His hair was deep black and almost curly, and, where his hat hadn't covered it, perspiration had left little channels in the dust that covered his neck and cheeks.

The shell belt that sagged from lean hips was of aged, softened leather, and the gun in the holster was anything but new. His age was thirty, and squint lines fanned out from his deepset blue eyes, under thick and dusty eyebrows.

Hat in hand, he opened the office door and was immediately in a long narrow room whose three desks were fenced off by a low railing with a swing gate in it. At the middle desk, a man of about his own age, wearing steel-rim glasses, glanced up from his work and said, almost with indifference, "What can I do for you?"

"I'm looking for Mr. Carpenter."

The clerk tilted his head to the far desk where a bulky man sat with his back to the railing and facing the far wall. At the sound of their voices, Jack Carpenter turned his swivel chair to

3

regard Cam. He was a rough, craggy-faced man, not recently shaven, and the hands resting on the chair arms were big and beaten.

He rose now and Cam saw he was not a tall man, but a wide one, dressed in careless work clothes and boots. His broad face held a deep reserve as he crossed over to the railing and halted before Cam.

"You can't be another of them bounty hunters, because you ain't drunk. What is it you want?"

"To make sure the stories I've heard aren't rumors," Cam said quietly.

"What have you heard, then?"

"That a week ago, the train was robbed of your bullion. That your son, guarding it, was killed. That the bullion was valued at nearly one hundred thousand dollars. That—"

"More than one hundred thousand," Carpenter interrupted.

"I heard you were offering half the bullion to anyone who could recover it and bring in your son's killer, too."

"Those aren't rumors. They're all facts. I don't reckon you've seen the posters I had printed up. The whole thing's there. Get somebody to read it to you."

Cam smiled faintly. "I think I can manage that. I think I can get your man, too."

"So does every bounty hunter in town, but they're looking in the wrong place. They won't find him at the bottom of a bottle of whiskey."

"I don't plan on looking there," Cam said. Then he added, "Take a good look at me, Mr. Carpenter. I'm the man you'll be paying."

Carpenter's glance held a faint contempt. "And you'd like a little advance on that money, is that right?"

"It won't be necessary," Cam said. Then he added gently, "I'm sorry about your son."

"Thanks," Carpenter said. He turned and went back to his desk, but not before Cam caught the shadow of grief on the broad face.

Cam went out, mounted, and put his gelding down the winding, rutted road that led on to El Cuervo's main street. He supposed that half of the bounty hunters, attracted by the huge reward, had badgered Carpenter into the testiness he had shown, but at least Cam had gotten the clarification he had wanted.

Now, going in, Cam looked at the town, which was a jumble of adobe buildings, tar-paper shacks, and tent dormitories. On the mountains that rose directly from the desert floor, he could see the headframes of the half-dozen mines, smoke coming from their boilers. They, and the stacks from the mill on the far edge of town, made a curtain of smoke that hung high over the valley.

Cam passed the roundhouse that was a terminus of the Arizona Central Railroad, moved past the frame depot, and was on El Cuervo's main street. It was busy with morning wagon and horse traffic, and as Cam moved through it he thought of the other things he needed to know about the robbery.

He had been moving his cattle up in the mountains to summer range a week ago when the robbery had taken place, and heard of it only from the sketchy report in the weekly newspaper at Indian Bend. The size of the reward was staggering in a country of poor towns and hard-scrabble ranches. Many of the sorry businesses in Indian Bend had closed up and their men had come to El Cuervo to join the hunt. The past dry winter with its stock losses in the falling market had hurt him, along with the other small ranchers. Since quitting the Big Ladder Ranch as foreman three years ago, and setting up on his own, things had been rough enough. But the losses of the winter had placed his holdings in real jeopardy. Half of Carpenter's bullion would make all the difference in his own precarious world.

Ahead of him now, he could see a crowd of men so large that it spilled out into the dusty street. The corner adobe building before which they were gathered had a portal stretching over the boardwalk, and, as Cam approached the crowd, he reined over to circle it. He was almost past them when he saw the sign saying "Sheriff's Office" over the door of the adobe building. Even as he was reading the sign, a half-dozen men came through the doorway to join the crowd. The last man out closed and locked the door and then moved over to the edge of the boardwalk. He raised both arms to quiet the crowd and Cam could see the star of the sheriff's office on his vest.

Cam reined up to listen as the sheriff began to speak.

When his gesture had quieted the crowd, the sheriff, a young-appearing, tall man with a scowl on his face, began to speak. "All right, you men, I know why all of you are here and I'm tired of telling you the same damn story from daylight to dark. This is the last time you'll hear it from me."

He started off sore, Cam thought, and he still looks sore.

The sheriff then described the robbery—the mistaken shooting of Dan Bowers by the brakeman and the killing of both bullion guards and the brakeman, who belatedly came into the baggage car. Only one man survived the shoot-out and nobody in the passenger car remembered him.

Someone in the crowd shouted, "What did they look like? Hell, a dozen people saw them."

Cam identified the speaker as a big man in dirty range clothes, his hat pushed to the back of his head to reveal a shock of thick pale blond hair, shades lighter than his weather-burned face.

"Here's the bunkhouse lawyer again," the sheriff said scornfully. "Well, Crowder, I talked to everybody in the car I could get ahold of. I get the same story. One man was taller than the other. They were dressed like most of you in the crowd here—stetson, neckerchief, shirt, pants, cowman's boots. Remember, the pair of them took the front seat in the car, so all anybody saw of them was their backs."

"What about Mrs. Bowers? She was closest to them," Crowder prodded.

"I'm coming to that, and you better listen. She gave the same description all the others did. Why would a happily married woman pay any attention to a couple of raunchy cowpokes—especially when she was with her husband?"

Crowder called out, "She already knew what he looked like.

She had to look at something, didn't she?" This brought a laugh from the crowd.

When they quieted, the sheriff went on. "Some of you have pestered that little lady until she's had to leave town. Even if you find her, she won't see you." He paused and said scathingly, "Why should a new, young widow be pestered by the likes of you? Besides, you know as much as she knows."

"Where was the train at when the gold was dumped?" somebody called.

"You all know that. At Calico Flats."

"Why didn't the train stop when it happened?" the man persisted.

"The engineer and fireman couldn't hear the shots. It was a long time before one of the passengers could make his way over the cars to tell the engineer what happened."

"What time of night was it?" a voice from the crowd called.

"The train left at nine o'clock and that's the last damn question I'll answer. But I've got something to say to all of you. Go back where you came from. There's a hundred bounty hunters here, bustin' into everybody's barns, trampin' down gardens, snoopin' where you don't belong, and pullin' a gun on every stranger that you don't like the looks of. Clear out of here and let the sheriff's office do its work."

"Why'd you send out them posters, if you didn't want us here?" Again, it was Crowder speaking.

"I had nothing to do with that," the sheriff said flatly. "That was Jack Carpenter's idea and he paid for the printing. Now go along, the whole lot of you, before I have to close up every saloon in town." The sheriff turned and went around the corner of the building, and now the crowd started to break up. More than half of them, Cam noted, headed for the Cameo Saloon across from the sheriff's office. Cam put his horse in motion and when he came to a building whose sign proclaimed *El Cuervo Times* he put his horse in to the tie rail and dismounted.

The door was open against the heat of the day. Inside, immediately ahead of him, was a high counter which stretched the width of the narrow room. Beyond it was a big square littered desk at which a girl sat facing an older man across the desk. The girl would be in her early twenties, Cam guessed, and her chestnut hair was pinned atop her head. She wore a blue dress with paper cuffs to protect the sleeves from the printer's ink that the whole hot room smelled of. Beyond the desk were the presses, typecases, composing stone, and cupboards.

The bald man seated across from the girl was the first to remark Cam's entrance, and, now, he spoke to the girl who rose and came over to face Cam across the counter. She was, Cam saw, a rather tall girl, full-bodied but not plump, and her oval face had a wide mouth, unsmiling now, below a faintly uptilted nose. Her eyes were dark and did not hold much friendliness as she said, "Something I can do for you?"

Cam nodded and said, "I'd like to see the paper that told the story about the gold robbery."

The girl sighed. "You and fifty other men." She tilted her head toward the end of the counter and said, "Come along." Cam followed her, the counter between them, until they came to the end of the counter where a copy of the *El Cuervo Times* was tacked down under a heavy piece of glass, held firmly by brackets.

The girl halted and asked, "Can you read?"

Cam looked down at the paper through the glass and said, "I get by, but I'm a little slow reading print upside down."

For the first time, the girl smiled. "So many of the bounty hunters can't read and I have to read it to them. You're another of them, aren't you?"

"I am, but you make it sound like a dirty word."

The girl looked at him levelly and said, "Isn't it? You're all out to kill a man for a lot of money, aren't you?"

"The man killed three men and caused the death of a fourth, but I suppose he's a likable cuss and we shouldn't be rough with him," Cam said dryly.

The girl flushed angrily, then pointed briefly to the counter gate against the wall. "Come through there and read it yourself," she said coldly, then turned and went back to the desk.

Cam came through the gate, halted before the glassed-over

Times, and read the account of the robbery. He also read the editorial deploring Jack Carpenter's invitation for any and all to join the manhunt. The masthead above the editorial said "William Cross, Editor and Publisher" and "Amelia Cross, Business Manager." There was nothing in the news story or editorial that Cam didn't already know, save for one item. Dan Bowers was a young El Cuervo lawyer and he and his wife were on their way to San Isbel to see a client of Dan's.

Cam finished reading and, his expression thoughtful, moved over to the girl and halted beside her. When she looked up from her proofreading, he said, "Can I ask you something, Miss Cross?"

At her nod, Cam glanced at the man who must be her father. A wet cigar lay on the edge of an ashtray heaped with cigar butts, and his shirt front was gray from the drift of cigar ashes. He had a wide mouth like his daughter, but the corners were downturned and his eyes seemed tired and cynical.

Cam asked of the girl, "Did anybody check Mrs. Bowers' story that she and her husband were on their way to see a client of his?"

William Cross spoke from across the table. "I did."

"How?"

"I telegraphed the town marshal in San Isbel and he confirmed the appointment."

"You'd have had to give him the name so he could check. What was the name?"

"Curly Fields. He got in some trouble over there, and the marshal wouldn't let him leave town."

Cam nodded, then spoke to the girl. "Why was Mrs. Bowers with her husband?"

"Why, Tina gets restless like most of the women in this town. There's not much here for them to do. A trip anywhere away from here is a treat."

"Tina?" Cam asked.

"Short for Christina."

"And where would I find her?"

"In the next house to ours usually, but you won't find her

there. And that's the end of the question period," the girl said tartly.

"Just supposing I run into her? What does she look like?"

William Cross answered, "That's easy. She's the prettiest girl you'll ever see."

Cam said gallantly, "You're wrong. I'm talking to her," and he looked at the girl. She blushed furiously and William Cross let out a raucous laugh. Furious and embarrassed, the girl rose and headed back into the shop.

"Much obliged," Cam said to Cross, and he turned to go.

"Hold on a minute, young fellow." When Cam halted, Cross said, "Who are you anyway? An insurance detective?"

Cam told his name and Cross rose and they shook hands. "No, I'm no detective. I'm just a near-broke rancher that needs the reward money to save his spread."

"Well, luck to you," Cross said. Cam nodded and started away and then halted. "Will you apologize for me to your daughter?"

Cross looked at him shrewdly. "To Amy? Of course not. What you said will set her up for a month, when she starts thinking it over."

Nodding, Cam grinned and left. Halting on the boardwalk, Cam considered what he'd learned. Both Cross and his daughter Amy were determined to protect Tina Bowers from the pestering of the bounty hunters. In their minds, her presence on the train was reasonable, and Bowers' errand in San Isbel had been checked out. But of all the passengers who got a look at the robbers, she was the closest. He must find her and talk to her, but where was he to look? The sheriff had told the crowd of bounty hunters that she had had to leave town. The station agent at the depot would probably know if she had taken a train, or a more likely source of information might be the bounty hunters themselves, who had been in town days longer than he had.

Remembering that most of the bounty hunters, dispersing after the chewing out from the sheriff, had gone across to the Cameo Saloon, Cam mounted and turned back down the street and put his horse in at the crowded tie rail in front of the big saloon.

Even as he headed for the bat-winged doors of the saloon, he could hear the racket inside. When he shouldered through the swinging doors, he was in a big, high-ceilinged, hot, smoke-filled room. The long bar on his left was jammed with men. The chairs around the three big poker tables to his right were all occupied by drinkers, and Cam was reminded of Carpenter's contempt for the bounty hunters as a group. Very likely they had already combed over the town and the surrounding country and were at a loss for where to look next.

There was a discussion down the bar which seemed to be attracting a good bit of attention from the bar patrons. Now, Cam shouldered his way through the crowd to see what was arousing their interest. A half-dozen men, with Crowder in the middle, were standing with their backs to the bar, drinks in hand, facing the curious crowd. Crowder seemed to be ending his speech, for he said, "All right, just talk it up. The more of us there are, the easier it'll be to swing it." He turned then and knocked his glass on the bar top for the bartender's attention, while the crowd broke up.

Cam moved up toward the bar and came in behind Crowder. He tapped the big man's shoulder and when Crowder turned his head Cam said, "I got in on the tail-end of it. Talk what up?"

Crowder straightened up, turned, and regarded him carefully. Face-to-face he seemed a bull of a man, with shoulders so wide they split the seams of his shirt at the top of the sleeves. His lips beneath a badly reset broken nose were tobacco stained, and he wore an arrogance in his amber-colored eyes like a banner.

"Ain't seen you around before," Crowder said, with only the slightest interest.

"I just got in," Cam said. "What is it you want talked up?"

"You alone, or you got a crew?" Crowder asked.

"I'm on my own."

This brought a derisive smile from Crowder, who looked at

one of his companions and said, "Hear that? We got a big loner here." Both men laughed.

"What's funny?" Cam asked mildly.

"Well, it's like you was born yesterday, mister. There's likely ten crews here, runnin' from five to a dozen, and I head one of 'em. That means I got six times the chance you have of finding the gold and the man that took it."

"Those aren't bad odds," Cam said mildly.

"No? Let's say you find where the gold's hid, and you get the jump on the man that hid it. You think I'll let you ride down this street without takin' that gold away from you? You think a dozen of these other crews will let you get away with it? That's why I brung my men and why the others brung theirs."

"When I find it, nobody'll take it away from me. They won't take my prisoner either," Cam said.

"Nobody takes anything from you. Is that what you're sayin'?" Crowder jeered.

"Nobody has yet," Cam said flatly.

Crowder's left arm was on the bar, and, now, watching him, Cam caught the warning twitch of a muscle in Crowder's neck. It was followed instantly by a sweeping drive of Crowder's left arm at Cam's midriff.

But the warning had been enough. Cam moved inside the swing and against Crowder, and, in the same motion, lifted a knee into Crowder's groin. Crowder gave a heavy grunt of pain and automatically bent over.

Cam took a half step to the left, then drove the fist of his left hand at a spot where Crowder's jaw hinge was buried in muscle. It was a solid blow that shocked Cam's arm clear to the shoulder. And even as Crowder was falling, caroming off his companion, Cam stepped back and lifted his gun out of its holster.

Crowder hit the floor with a thud, then slowly rolled over on his face.

Slowly Cam backed away as the six men in Crowder's crew watched. When he had some of the bar patrons between him and the crew, he turned and walked out of the saloon.

On the boardwalk, outside, a couple of cowpunchers were discussing something as Cam came up to them. They ceased talking and Cam said, "Either of you hear what Crowder was saying in there?"

The taller of the two, a weather-burned, middle-aged man, said, "Yeah, that's what we was talking about. This Crowder found out Dan Bowers had a sister. She's married to a fellow calls himself Lew Kimball. He owns the Diamond K, about three miles east of town. Crowder figures Miz Bowers headed for there."

"Why'd Crowder tell the whole saloon about it?" Cam asked.

"Well, looks like this Kimball has a pretty hefty crew. Crowder figured the crew couldn't fight off fifty men so he wants us to gang up and go out there and have our talk with Miz Bowers."

"You buying the idea?" Cam asked.

The puncher shrugged. "Why not? I don't know who I'm looking for, and she's the only one that knows what he looks like."

"When are you going?"

"Soon's Crowder can get enough men to scare the Diamond K crew. I don't reckon it'll take long, because all of us want to know what that killer looks like."

"Me too," Cam said. "Thanks."

Cam found his horse, mounted, and rode down the street as far as the feed stable where a hostler was lounging against the entrance to the runway. From him, Cam got the directions on how to find the Diamond K, and minutes later he had left El Cuervo behind him. He hoped that Crowder unwittingly had provided him access to Tina Bowers, but, then, perhaps someone else who had heard Crowder had the same thought he had. However, it was worth the try.

The country he was traveling through was a hilly desert of mesquite and cactus, and the sparse bunchgrass he saw made him wonder if it wouldn't take a hundred acres to feed one cow.

When he came to the first side road he took it. A hundred

13

yards down it, he saw it would take him between two mesquite-covered hills. As he approached the cleft between the hills, two riders came out from the thick mesquite into the open. They both had rifles across their saddles.

Cam approached them and reined in, asking, "This the right way to the Diamond K?"

"Could be," one of the guards said. "What'd you want there?"

"To talk to Lew Kimball."

"What about?" the other guard asked.

"There's trouble on the way," Cam said quietly.

"Like what?" the first guard asked.

"Like maybe fifty—seventy-five men."

The two guards looked at each other and the first guard said, "Tell us about it."

"No, I'll tell Kimball."

"You sure you will?" the second guard asked sardonically.

Before Cam could answer, the first guard said, "Take his gun and let him through, Harry. If he's trouble, the boys can handle him."

Cam surrendered his gun and was passed on. Beyond the hills he could see ahead of him a tall stand of cottonwoods in the middle of which was a one-story, sprawling adobe building. Behind him, to the west of these towering trees, lay the bunkhouse, outbuildings, and corrals. As approached, he could hear the clang of someone working at an anvil and the sound seemed to come from an adobe building next to the open-faced wagon shed.

As he headed toward the adobe, whose double doors were open, he looked at the ranch house. It was a big U-shaped affair with a patio in the middle holding plantings that were a riot of color. As he passed it, he saw two children watching from the patio, and no sooner had he seen them than one, a girl, disappeared into the house.

Reining in in front of the open doors of the dimly lit blacksmith shop, he could make out the figure of a man, who, now seeing him, ceased his hammering and came out into the sunlight, a big hammer still in his hand.

"I'm looking for Lew Kimball."

"You're talking to him," the man said.

Kimball was a man in his forties, stocky, round-faced, almost bald, and dressed in worn range clothes. His tone was pleasant enough, but his dark eyes held a certain wariness. As Cam swung out of the saddle, he was aware of two men approaching from the bunkhouse and of the boy he had seen at the house, running toward him.

Moving up to Kimball, Cam halted and said, "You don't know me, Kimball. Name's Cam Holgate."

Kimball frowned and did not offer to shake hands. Cam observed that Kimball was noting his empty holster as he said, "What can I do for you?"

"Why, just listen, I reckon." Cam heard the sound of running feet and then the boy came up to stand beside Kimball, who put a hand on his shoulder.

"This is my son, Joey, Mr. Holgate." Both Cam and the boy nodded and smiled at each other and then Kimball said, "What am I to listen to?"

Cam heard a sound behind him, looked over his shoulder, and saw two cowpunchers standing a few feet away. And, now hearing a door slam, he looked over at the house. Two women and the girl he had seen before were walking toward the blacksmith shop. Cam looked at Kimball and smiled faintly.

"Maybe I'd better wait till everybody's here."

Kimball smiled faintly too and said, "Everybody thinks if my men let you through, they'd like to know why."

"They won't like the reason and neither will you, but I suppose you all should know."

Cam turned his head to look at the two women and the girl approaching. He assumed the older woman, a plain, pleasant-looking woman, was the mother of the two children. The younger woman couldn't be anybody else but Tina Bowers, for, as William Cross had put it, she was the prettiest girl he'd ever see. She was smaller than Mrs. Kimball and not even the divided skirt and man's shirt she was wearing could hide the full perfection of her figure. Her auburn hair was turned to copper by the sunlight. As the three of them approached and halted, Cam noted the features that added up to William Cross's description of Tina. Her eyes were of the clearest blue, wide-spaced, under straight brows. If fair skin went with auburn hair, then this was a contradiction, for she had a dark complexion without freckles, with a faint glow of color at her high cheekbones. Her nose was faintly aquiline and her lips were both straight and full. She couldn't help but be aware of her looks and her figure, yet Cam's appraisal seemed to faintly embarrass her.

Kimball made the introductions, and afterward said, "Mr. Holgate has some news for us."

Cam then explained what Crowder had been talking up in the saloon. When he mentioned the number of crews Crowder had spoken about, Tina Bowers' lips parted in surprise and she looked at Kimball.

"That adds up to over fifty men, Lew," Tina said.

Kimball nodded and said bitterly, "Against six of us."

"Seven, if you count me," Cam said.

"Thanks," Kimball said, and then added, "but why are you here? Why'd you come?"

"Two reasons," Cam said. "First, I can't see fifty men bullying one woman. The second is, I'm one of the bounty hunters."

"What does that last mean?"

"I reckon you'd call it favor for favor. I've warned you what's coming. Does that earn me the right to talk to Mrs. Bowers alone?"

Kimball looked at his sister-in-law. "That's for you to answer, Tina."

Tina was watching Cam and now she said, "How do we know you didn't make this up?"

"You don't know," Cam said and left it there.

Mrs. Kimball then spoke for the first time. "What do you suggest we do, Mr. Holgate?"

"Why, tell them Mrs. Bowers is gone and let five men search the place to prove it."

"But, where'll we hide Tina?" Mrs. Kimball asked.

"I heard the sheriff tell the bounty hunters this morning that Mrs. Bowers had left town. Why not send her back to her own house until this is over? They won't look there."

Lew Kimball said, "What do I tell that gang of bounty hunters?"

"Have you got a line camp?"

"Three of them."

"Tell them she's at the farthest one."

"And when they don't find her they'll come back."

"It'll give you time to get the sheriff here with some deputies."

Apparently Kimball had made up his mind. He turned and said to one of the two men who had been listening, "Harv, ride down to the boys and tell 'em to fire two quick shots when this mob comes in sight. Then they're to get back here." Then he looked at Tina Bowers. "Made up your mind, girl?"

"Yes, I'll talk to him," Tina said. "Come into the house."

After leaving his horse at the house tie rail Cam followed Tina across the patio and into a large comfortable living room containing deep leather-covered chairs and a long leather-covered sofa facing a stone fireplace. Indian rugs were scattered at random on the Mexican tile floors.

Tina gestured to Cam to sit on the sofa while she sat down in one of the chairs to the side of it. They regarded each other warily before Tina said, "Exactly what is it you want to know?"

"This can't be very pleasant for you, Mrs. Bowers. Why don't I tell you what I know about it and you stop me when I'm wrong." At her nod, he started with the wait at the station. Did she watch the loading of the gold bullion?

"Why yes. I never knew how it was done. I'd heard, but I'd never seen it." She shrugged her shapely shoulders. "It wasn't much."

"Were the other passengers watching?"

"A woman with a little boy."

"But the sheriff said you were seated on the train before the robbers came past you. That meant they had watched it too. Did you see them on the platform? You noticed the woman and boy. Why not them?"

She shrugged. "It's not the same thing. A woman always looks at another woman. Maybe they bought their tickets later."

In spite of her assured answers, Cam sensed a certain uneasiness, a hint of evasiveness in her manner.

Cam continued, "All right, you were sitting down next to the window when the two men passed your husband and sat down. Did you get a look at their faces?"

"Their backs were to me. No"

"Did they talk to each other?"

She hesitated and then said, "I—I think so."

"Then they must have turned their heads so you could see their profiles."

"But I didn't pay them any attention. I think one man had a mustache but they both needed shaves."

"Which man had the mustache—the tall man on the aisle seat or the one next to the window?"

"The man next to the window."

"Was there anything unusual about their clothes?"

"No. That's just it. They were dressed like you only they wore dirty jackets over their shirts."

"Any marks or scars you could see on either one?"

"I tell you I didn't look at them that much. Why should I?"

Cam said in the same tone of patience, "Mrs. Bowers, do you want your husband's killer found?"

"Why, his killer was the brakeman and he's dead," Tina said impatiently.

"But the man responsible for getting him killed is alive. Do you want him found?"

"That's a foolish question. Of course I do!"

"Then remember, remember," Cam said gently.

"But I can't!" Tina said, almost angrily.

"How was he different from me?"

Tina thought a moment, then said, "Not so tall, but heavier built. Not so brown-faced."

"His hair?"

"Not so dark." She paused. "That's all I can remember."

"All right." Cam paused, marshaling his thoughts, then he asked, "You and your husband heard the shots, the sheriff told us."

"Yes."

"Why didn't your husband go after the robbers right then? Why did he wait until the brakeman ran past him?"

"He thought the two men were fighting and nobody walks into a gunfight. When the brakeman ran past us he caught on that there was trouble in the baggage car and tried to help." She dabbed at her beautiful eyes with her handkerchief and murmured, "It was so foolish, plain foolish."

As she finished speaking Cam heard through the doorway the two distant signal shots. They both rose now and were headed for the patio when they heard the sound of running feet. Joey rounded the corner of the house, saw them come out and called, "They're coming, Aunt Tina!"

Tina picked up her hat from one of the patio chairs. Cam said, "Take my horse, Mrs. Bowers. He's right here by the house and saddled. Leave him at the feed stable and tell the hostler to grain him."

As they rounded the corner of the house and approached the tie rail they saw Kimball jogging toward them. By the time Kimball had reached them, Cam had given Tina a leg up and she was in the saddle.

Cam was handing her the reins when Kimball halted beside him. Breathing hard he said, "Go ahead, Tina. Harv was in such a hurry he left the corral gate open and the horses scattered." He looked down the road and said, "Hurry it, girl. Cut around the house and head north. We'll be in to see you."

They watched as Tina, on Cam's horse, cut around the back of the house and disappeared. Kimball looked at him and said, "Get what you wanted?"

"I don't know," Cam said. "I do know I'm no good to you without a gun."

"Get a carbine and load it, Joey," Kimball said, and the boy was off to the kitchen door.

Kimball turned to Cam then and said, "I'm putting Abbie and the twins in the bunkhouse with one of my men—you."

"I'm the wrong man, Kimball. I'm apt to draw lightning from Crowder."

"I'd forgotten that. All right, you fort up in the kitchen. I'll meet them right outside the kitchen door."

Now Cam saw the crew, four men with rifles, leave the cookshack next to the bunkhouse and head for the house. Apparently they already had their orders, for they headed for the kitchen door. Kimball intercepted them and sent one man back to the bunkhouse. Joey came out then, handed Cam a carbine, and ran for the bunkhouse.

As the man turned back Cam looked down the road. In the distance he saw the vanguard of the bounty hunters. The two Diamond K guards were leading with the bounty hunters following, and while Cam couldn't count them at this distance he judged there were more than fifty mounted men in the pack.

Now Cam headed for the kitchen in front of whose door Kimball stood, also watching the approaching mob. When Cam reached him he raised a hand to halt him. Cam saw the beads of perspiration on his face and he knew Kimball was afraid and Cam didn't blame him.

"I've never handled anything like this. What do I do?"

"That makes two of us," Cam said. "Still, I'll make a guess. Ask who their leader is and talk only to him. Let him pick the five-man search party and you go with them. Tell him if there's trouble your men will fire into the mob."

"All right," Kimball said grimly.

Cam moved past him and into the kitchen, a big room holding a large table with chairs, a black iron stove, a cooler, cupboards, sink and counter pump beside it. Moving to a curtained window by the table Cam drew the curtains slightly and waited. He picked up the muffled sound of many horses walking. The sound increased until Kimball called sharply, "Stop right there."

The sound slowly eased off and then Kimball moved into Cam's line of vision and halted. Kimball's two guards, dismounted now, came up to stand beside him.

"Who do I talk to?" Kimball asked angrily.

"You don't talk to nobody, Kimball. We talk to you."

Sure enough, it was Crowder's voice.

"Come over here," Kimball ordered.

Pushing the curtain aside Cam got his first look at the mob. The members of it were of all sizes and descriptions, mounted on horses, mules, even burros. There were wagons and buckboards and buggies.

Cam saw Crowder in the front line of riders put his horse in motion and rein in in front of Kimball.

"All right, talk," Kimball said.

"We come out to talk to Mrs. Bowers. Bring her out."

"I know why you've come, and I made sure she wouldn't be here."

"Where is she?" Crowder asked.

"I have three line camps. She's at one of them."

There was an angry murmur of protest from the men who could hear Kimball.

"Which one, and where is it?" Crowder demanded.

"I left the choice up to the man who took her. I told him not to tell me where he was taking her. As for where the line camps are, *you* find them."

"You'll show us, by God!" a new voice called.

"You bounty hunters have six rifles trained on you right now. You make a move toward me and you're dead."

Crowder said coldly, "You're lying, Kimball. She's in the house. We're going to talk to her if we have to tear the place apart. You may get some of us but we'll get you and your men."

While Crowder was talking the bounty hunters moved their horses to encircle Kimball, and Kimball saw it.

"All right, search the place. But only five of you," Kimball said. "I'll show you our whole layout, but only five of you."

"We all look!" a whiskey-slurred voice shouted.

Cam raised his rifle and shot over Crowder's head. A couple of horses shyed and Cam called out, "Just five of you, like Kimball says."

A rider moved his horse up to Crowder and said, "I'll be one of the five, Bill."

This brought an angry comment from another man and a murmur of protest ran among the crowd.

Kimball raised his arms and called, "Hold it! Hold it!" When the men quieted, he said, "What does it matter which five? If she's in there she'll be brought out for all of you to talk to."

"You're damn right she will!" a man called.

Kimball said to Crowder, "Will you pick them or will I?"

"You," Crowder answered.

Kimball pointed three times, saying, "You, you, and you," to three different men.

Crowder and the four men dismounted and now Kimball led them around the corner of the house, heading for the patio and the living room. Cam, from his place in the kitchen, could hear them opening doors and closing them, moving furniture and shifting it back, opening wardrobes and shutting them.

The steps of the six men came from the pantry and then Kimball came in, followed by Crowder and the others, Kimball's crew following.

"You've seen every room but this and there's no place to hide here," Kimball said.

Crowder didn't answer. He was looking at Cam and the rifle he held, a look of surprise, recognition, and then anger on his heavy face.

"You work for Kimball?" he asked.

"Right now I do."

"So you're the one that tipped him off." At Cam's nod he said, "And you talked with her."

Kimball said, "Tina was gone before Holgate got here. I figured you bounty hunters would come out here, but I didn't know when."

"Holgate," Crowder said softly, as if to engrave it in memory. Then he looked about the room, saw there was no place to hide, then said, "All right. Let's look at the other buildings."

They filed out of the kitchen door but Cam kept his station. As they passed the bounty hunters Crowder called, "She's not in there, boys."

The barn was searched first, then the wagon shed, blacksmith's shop, and cookshack. Kimball halted before the bunkhouse and said, "My wife and children are in there but go ahead and look."

The other bounty hunters followed Kimball into the big hot room which held double-deck bunks on two sides. Abbie Kimball and the children were seated on a bench flanking a big table littered with newspapers, ore samples, cards, and a checkerboard. The stale air of the room smelled of unwashed clothes and sweat.

Abbie Kimball said, "Can we go now, Lew? It's stifling in here."

Kimball nodded and Abbie headed for the door, the twins following. Elli halted in the doorway, turning to see where the search crew would look.

Crowder was the closest to her and he said, "Hello, missy. We're looking for your aunt."

"She's gone."

"Did she go in a buggy?"

"No. That nice man loaned her his horse. Ours got out of the corral."

"What nice man?"

"The one that came before all of you did. He was riding a horse with a funny brand like a hatchet."

"Did he talk with your aunt?"

Kimball from the far end of the room called, "Elli, run along now."

The little girl turned and ran to catch up with her mother and brother. Watching her, Crowder smiled. She had no idea what she had just told him. If Holgate had given Mrs. Bowers his horse, then he must have talked with her.

When the bunkhouse search was ended the bounty hunters,

still under guard, returned to the mob who had scattered to the shade of the cottonwoods where many of them were drinking from bottles they had brought. As Crowder approached they gathered to hear him.

Crowder said to them, "We looked everywhere and she's gone."

Cam, still at his station, heard him. This was the time that held the greatest danger. The bounty hunters, disappointed, many of them drunk, all responsible to nobody, could vent their anger on the Kimballs. It came as a surprise then when he heard Crowder raise his voice. "All right, let's go and leave these people alone."

"We could take one of them kids until they give us Mrs. Bowers," a man called.

"Go ahead. You'll only have seven men shootin' at you. Me, I'm gettin' out of here."

Crowder mounted and his crew fell in behind him and they headed down the road into the lowering sun. Grumbling and cursing, the rest began to follow him.

Kimball stood watching, one of his crew on either side of him, as the last rider mounted and headed out. Cam tramped out and halted beside him.

"What got into Crowder, I wonder?" Cam said. "He started out salty and wound up talking sense."

"Thank God for that," Kimball said. "That was about as squeaky as they come." He extended his hand now and Cam accepted it. "I want to thank you for the warning. It made the difference." Then he added, "You want to work for me, Holgate?"

Cam shook his head. "I'm still bounty hunting, Kimball. All I'd like is the loan of a horse to get me back to town."

2

It was almost dusk when Cam rode back into El Cuervo and, picking his way through the ceaseless wagon traffic, he passed the *El Cuervo Times* office. Seeing there were lamps lit inside he put his horse into the tie rail, dismounted, and tramped back to the newspaper office.

Looking through the window he saw both William and Amy Cross at work in the shop. Amy was at the typecase, stick in hand, while her father was at the stone with the forms atop it. Both were working under the light cast by a shaded overhead lamp while a second man watched Cross.

Cam tried the door, found it unlocked, went inside, passed through the gate, and went back into the shop. Cross was first to hear him and looked up as Cam stepped into the circle of lamplight. Cross grinned and said, "Well, the bounty hunter's back. Find your gold?"

Amy turned at the sound of her father's voice. She was wearing an ink-stained apron over her dress and paper cuffs above her wrists. At the sight of him she smiled faintly.

"Not yet," Cam said. "I saw your lamp lit and figured to ask you some questions."

"You already have, but go ahead," Amy said.

The second man was the young sheriff, Cam noted, and they exchanged nods.

"Would you know who got that dead train robber ready for burial?"

"Why there's only one undertaker here," Amy said. "That's

25

Andy Johnson at Johnson's hardware two doors down." She pointed with her stick of type.

"Why do you want to know, fella?" the sheriff asked.

He was about Cam's height, hatless, and the overhead lamp brought out the planes in his long face. His hair, worn long, was a chestnut color as were his mustaches over a wide mouth. He had a quiet belligerence about him that Cam supposed was triggered by Cross's calling Cam a bounty hunter.

"To find out what he looked like."

"And what good will that do you? He's underground. Besides, it's the other man you want the description of and you won't get it."

"I'll get it, sheriff," Cam said. "Sheriff who?"

Cross said, "Sheriff Ben Judd. And Ben, this is Cam Holgate."

Both men nodded again; neither offered to shake hands.

"How'll you get it?" the sheriff scoffed.

"I don't know yet," Cam said simply, and he looked at Amy. "If you're working tonight that must mean the *Times* will be out tomorrow."

"That's right," Amy said.

"Anybody tell you what happened out at Diamond K this afternoon?"

"I told her," Judd said.

"Were you there?" Cam asked.

"No. I heard about it."

"Why weren't you there?" Cam asked. "Kimball could sure of used you."

"I didn't know it was going to happen."

"I did. Just by asking on the street." He nodded to Cross, said, "Thanks," looked coolly at the angry Judd, then turned and walked out.

When the door closed Judd looked at Cross. "Don't he know people clam up to the law?"

"Maybe not."

"Who is he?"

"First, I thought he was a railroad detective but he said not. Just another bounty hunter."

"He'll stand some watching," Judd said sullenly.

Cross said dryly, "He told Amy this morning she was the prettiest girl he'll ever see."

"Dad!" Amy said hotly.

"He said that?" Judd asked angrily. He stood up and started out of the circle of lamplight, headed for the door. "Nobody going to say that to my girl."

"Hold it," Cross said, and Judd halted and looked back at him. Cross then told him about Cam's curiosity about Tina's looks, his answer, and Cam's flattering appraisal: then he added, "How would he know she was your girl?"

"She was wearing my ring."

"She'd just come from the shop and she doesn't wear it there because it might get hung up in the press and she'd, get hurt. You know that. So he didn't see any ring. So don't you go off half-cocked."

The sheriff looked over at Amy and grinned sheepishly. "All right, but he better watch his mouth."

Cam found Johnson's hardware store still open. Several miners just off day shift were making purchases, which probably accounted for the late store hours.

Cam picked out the oldest of the three clerks and waited until his customer had been served and departed.

The heavyset balding man wearing iron-rimmed glasses moved over to him, saying pleasantly, "What can I get you?"

"You Mr. Johnson, the undertaker?" At Johnson's nod Cam asked, "You laid out that train robber that was killed?"

"I prepared all four bodies," Johnson said with dignity.

"I'm only interested in the holdup man. You buried him in the clothes he wore, didn't you?"

"He had no others."

"Can you describe the shirt he was wearing?"

Johnson didn't have to think. "It must've started out a red

checked calico, but the sun had faded it to a sort of salmon color."

"But you could still see the checks?"

"If you were close enough."

"Did you examine the body? What I mean is, did he have any identifying marks on him?"

Johnson thought only a moment. "Two. His left hand had been broken and the fingers badly reset. The other was a red scar—a knife scar, I'd judge—on the back of his neck."

Cam tried to keep the elation from his voice as he asked, "Did his hair hide it?"

"Only part of it. Most of it showed."

"Could you see it from, say, four feet away?"

"Easily." He frowned now for the first time. "Why do you want to know?"

"One more question. Did he wear mustaches?"

"No. He hadn't shaved for a while but he didn't have mustaches."

"Reason I'm asking is I think I saw this fellow with another man. He could be the one that got away with the gold."

"Is that so? Well, if you remember what the other man looked like you better tell the sheriff."

Cam nodded. "Much obliged to you, Mr. Johnson."

"But you won't, will you?"

"That's right," Cam said, smiled, and tramped through the store and out the door.

Cam rode his borrowed horse down to the feed stable, left word he'd be called for, and tramped back to the Montezuma Hotel and signed for a room opening on a flower-filled patio; there he stripped off his shirt and began to wash up.

As he lathered his torso and face, he summed up in his mind the information Johnson had given him. As close as Tina had been to the dead robber on the train, she couldn't have helped but observe the knife scar on his neck, and his checked and salmon-colored shirt. She had lied about the mustache. In fact, she had lied so much that Cam was sure that she knew the live bullion robber. He was equally sure that Dan Bowers had intended to join the holdup men in their attack on the guards. Why was she lying?

There could be only one reason, Cam thought. She was protecting the identity of the robber so she could demand her husband's share of the bullion from him.

3

Once he was cleaned up, Cam felt a vast impatience to see Tina again. However, he would have to wait until full dark to go to her house, and besides, he hadn't eaten since breakfast.

He went out onto the busy street and made his way through off-shift miners until he found a café next to the Cameo. It was crowded with bounty hunters and oven hot from body heat, but he found a place, after first paying for his meal, on a bench at a long table under an overhead lamp. The service was family style with great platters of meat, vegetables, and bread.

He wolfed down his meal and was packing his pipe, looking around the room jammed with half-drunk, hungry men. He was aware now of a man across and down the table studying him carefully. When he met the man's gaze, it shifted to his plate. He'd seen that face today, but then he'd seen fifty faces.

Abruptly now, the man rose, stepped over the bench, and began to elbow his way through the crowd to the door. And then Cam had it. This was one of the men siding Crowder at the bar and at the confrontation with Kimball later. Cam looked at the man's plate and it was half full. The sight of Cam had been important enough for him to leave his meal half finished and seek the street. And seek out Crowder too?

Cam rose, caution pushing him. Instead of heading for the street, he turned and headed for the kitchen. A couple of Mexican cooks and a half-dozen Mexican waitresses paid him only the briefest attention as he made his way through the room and stepped out of the open back door into full dark.

As he found the alley and followed it back behind the Cameo he wondered why his presence would be important to Crowder. Did Crowder suspect he had seen Tina before the bounty hunters reached Diamond K in spite of Kimball's lie? It didn't really matter, for in a few minutes' time he would have what he wanted from Tina. Reaching the street he made sure he was not followed, then questioned a townsman about the Cross house where Amy had said Tina lived next to her. He got directions and followed them to a side street where two houses, much alike in the night, stood isolated. The first house had lamps lit; the other house was dark and Cam knew this one must be the Bowers house, since Tina would not dare light a lamp to attract bounty hunters. In the darkness he could make out only that it was of frame.

Circling the house now he came up the steps to the back porch, moved across it and knocked softly on the door. "It's me, Tina, Cam Holgate. Let me in."

Cam heard a movement behind the door and then Tina's muffled voice from behind the thick door called, "Who is it?"

"It's Cam, and I have to talk to you."

"Just a minute," she called. Cam waited, there was absolutely no light to see by. He knew the door was being opened only because of a squeaking hinge.

"I haven't dared to light a lamp," Tina said. "Follow me, if you can see me. I can't see you."

"Lead on, I can just make you out."

He moved inside and heard a whisper of cloth to the side of him. And then the whole world seemed to land atop his head. He never was to remember falling.

"Did you get him?" Tina asked.

"Like I never got one before."

"Can he hear us?"

"Not for a long time."

"Well, we're in this together now, Wes, where *is* the bullion?"

"Like I told you. It's where I hid it."

"Aren't you going to give me Dan's share?"

31

"You're not very bright, sweetie. Why should I split with you? What did you do to earn it?"

"I could always turn you over to the sheriff, Wes. Have you thought of that?"

"You wouldn't and couldn't open your mouth to him; you're as involved in the killing of those men as I am."

"I can write an anonymous letter involving you."

"Two can play at that game, honey. Let's face it. You can ace me and I can pull you down with me. But you won't do it. Not unless you like jail better than I do."

"Where is the bullion?"

He ignored the question since he had already answered it. "What did you tell this Holgate this afternoon?"

"Nothing that would make him suspect I knew anything."

"Then why's he here now?"

"I don't know. It was his idea that I came back here. Maybe he wanted to see if I was."

"I think I ought to take him out and dump him down a prospect hole."

"Where would that get you?" Tina asked. "Everybody knows he talked to me—Lew and Abbie and the crew. If anything happens to him they come right back at me. Besides he doesn't know who or what you look like."

"What are you stickin' up for him for?"

"I'm not sticking up for him," Tina said hotly. "I'm just trying to keep out of more trouble."

"You'd better keep me out of that trouble, too."

"That's what I'm trying to do, can't you see?"

"What does he look like?"

"Strike a match and find out."

Swearing, Chance fumbled in his clothing for a match, found Cam, knelt beside him, and wiped the match alight.

It occurred to Tina, watching him, that both men were of widely contrasting types—Cam, lean and gaunt-looking, lying there with a pool of blood beneath his cheek. Wes Chance was stocky and bull-like with a heavy head and a sullen, cruel face.

Chance let the match die and then rose. "What are you going to tell him when he asks why he got rapped over the head?"

"That a man was courting me and that he was surprised and mad at being interrupted."

"And what was his name?"

"I'll make one up."

"Just see that it isn't Wes Chance."

Chance moved toward the back door and hearing him move Tina asked, "Where are you going?"

"It doesn't matter," Chance said easily.

"Will I see you again?"

"Not here, maybe on the street. But sure not here."

"Then I get nothing, nothing at all for protecting you?"

"That's right, honey. But that's not what you'll get if you don't protect me. You'll get jail. That ought to interest you. And look, no more street kids with notes hunting me down. It's risky and besides I'll be gone." He went out, closing the door behind him.

Now Tina stepped around Cam and groped her way to the stove which was still warm from the supper she had cooked on it after darkness had fallen. As she fumbled around for a basin to fill with water from the teakettle, her anger at Wes Chance was total. She had protected him all the days she had spent at Diamond K, and then today, her first time alone, when she had summoned him to arrange for her share of the bullion, he had not only refused to share it but laughed at her.

She filled the basin with warm water, found a cloth, and felt her way back to where Cam was lying. Kneeling beside him, but still not touching him, she wondered what she was doing. Why not leave him here? To be found and arrested as a prowler who had broken into her house. Still, to the sheriff this would seem strange and improbable. No, the thing to do was help him so he could get out and leave her alone.

As she began to probe for the source of the blood she had seen on the floor, she must have touched a sensitive spot, for he groaned and moved away from her hands, murmuring, "Tina, Tina."

"I'm here. Now sit up and hold still and let me wash that cut."

Cam obeyed silently, sitting up and wincing as she washed the cut atop his head; it throbbed painfully with every beat of his heart. When she was finished she said, "Do you feel well enough to walk out on your own?"

He rose unsteadily to his feet, caught his balance, and anchored himself against a chair. "Not just yet, Tina. We have some talking to do."

"I can't imagine what about. We're talked out."

"Who hit me when I came in?"

"A friend of mine, a sort of beau; he didn't like being interrupted. Now why don't you go before he comes back?"

"How did he know you were here?"

"I sent for him."

"Still another lie."

"Another? What was the other one?"

"There were lots of them, Tina, and you know it. Do you want me to name them?"

"If you can," Tina said almost jeeringly.

"All right. Take this afternoon. First you said you didn't notice anything strange about either of the men in the seat ahead of you. You're lying, because the short man had a red scar on the back of his neck. You couldn't have helped but see it unless you were blind, and you aren't. He wore a salmon-colored shirt, checked, but you didn't notice that either, you said."

"What's this supposed to prove?" Her voice was still brave and Cam wished he could see her face.

"You lied about not noticing anything remarkable about him, so it figures you're lying about the other man. You gave a wrong description of him, I'm sure. You said he was tall and I'm betting he's middle height. I'm betting he has a mustache." Cam paused. "You have only one reason for covering up for him. He has the bullion and you want your husband's share of it. I'm betting he's the man that buffaloed me. I'm betting you were talking over the split when I knocked on the door."

"It's you that's lying!" Tina said hotly. "You're making that up about the man with the scar and the salmon-colored shirt. You're making it all up, hoping to trap me! How did you know about the scar?"

"The undertaker, Tina."

"Why wouldn't the sheriff have noticed it?"

"I reckon the man was laid out on his back when the sheriff had his look at him. Probably he had a canvas pulled up over him, how could the sheriff see the scar. Now do you admit you lied?"

Tina did not answer and Cam guessed he had her on the run. He said quietly, "You've trapped yourself, Tina, and you know it."

"I'll stick by my story," Tina said coldly.

"All right. I'm going to the sheriff right now with a true description of the short man. He'll call you in and ask the same questions I've asked. What'll you answer?"

"I'll—I'll stick to my story."

"Want to try it?"

There was a long silence and then Tina said faintly, "No."

"Want to tell me the whole story, Tina?"

"If I do, how will you use it? Are you a law officer?"

"I'm just what I claim to be, a bounty hunter. What you can tell me I'll use to get back the bullion."

"Will you give me some of it if you do?"

A swift elation came to Cam then. Her very question told him much. If the bullion robber had agreed to share any part of the loot with her she would never have asked the question. Instead she would have asked for time to think about it and then got in touch with the bullion robber to have him get rid of Cam.

Now Cam said quietly, "He won't share with you, will he?"

"No, damn him! But will you?"

"Yes. A tenth of the reward."

"That's nothing," Tina said scornfully.

"It's a lot more than nothing, and I'll be the one to capture

35

it, you won't. Besides you're in no position to bargain with me, are you?"

He heard Tina sigh and finally she said, "Women always get the short end of every bargain. But I'll take it."

He heard a rustle of cloth as she came nearer to him and then she said, "A bargain has to be sealed by something, doesn't it?"

"Like a lawyer drawing up a contract?" Cam asked dryly.

"We can't do that, but we can do this."

Suddenly she moved against him and he felt her arms around his neck. Now her face was searching for his and his lips and when she kissed him he could not help but feel a thrust of excitement. Her body was soft against him and her lips were warm and loose and sweet. Before he could respond in any way she stepped away from him.

"Does that seal the bargain?" she asked.

"Very pleasantly," Cam said, and heard her low almost lewd laugh.

"Now tell it from the beginning," Cam said.

"There's a kitchen table with chairs against the wall. Why don't we sit down?"

Cam already had his chair and now he moved around it and sat down. He heard Tina draw her chair close to his. When she started to speak, he realized she was so close to him that he could feel the warm glow of her body. She sighed almost imperceptibly and began talking.

"Dan was doing no good here and we were in debt. He's the one that had the idea of robbing the bullion. Wes Chance—he's the one that was here tonight—is a small-time horse trader that Dan defended for horse stealing. Wes sent outside for Billy Weaver, the third man. He's the dead man."

Calmly, she went on to explain that while Dan had traveled the train rarely, neither Chance nor Weaver had ever ridden it, so there was no danger of their being recognized by the brakeman. It wasn't hard to pick up from the millhands when a bullion shipment was due to go out. The chanciest part of the plan was that Tom Carpenter would recognize Dan. Thus

Weaver and Chance had to go first into the baggage car and kill Carpenter and the other bullion guard, then the three of them would shove the bullion out the door and Weaver and Chance would jump after it. Dan would remain on the train. He would claim that he had a shot at one of the men but that he didn't think he hit him. Everyone knew now how that plot had failed. Of everyone in the scheme only she and Chance were alive. Chance knew where the gold was, but he refused to share it with her. She couldn't turn him in to the sheriff or he would turn around and betray her.

As she talked Cam felt a touch of nausea rise in him. Here this most beautiful of women was talking about murder as if it were no more important than choosing a good quality of cloth for a dress.

When she was finished, Cam asked coldly, "Did you love your husband, Tina?"

"While he was here," she said practically. "But he's gone and I have to live."

The female of the species, Cam thought sourly. He said then, "All right, back to Wes Chance. Describe him and tell me everything you know about him."

4

Amy and Sheriff Judd watched the train pull out, carrying this week's edition of the *El Cuervo Times* down the valley, and then the sheriff handed Amy up into the seat of the buckboard and joined her.

Heading down the busy main street Amy was mostly silent, for press day was always wearying. Approaching the Cameo they could hear the racket booming out from inside and Amy said, "That would be the bounty hunters, wouldn't it?"

"Their money has to run out sometime," Judd said wryly.

"Are there still as many of them?"

"More, if anything."

Amy was silent a moment and then she said, "I suppose if I'd lost a son like Jack Carpenter did I'd have put up that big reward money. Still, all it's done is bring most of the riffraff in the Southwest into this town."

Ben nodded and they were silent until he pulled up the buckboard in front of Amy's lighted house. He was about to get down and hand her down when she put a hand on his knee.

"Don't get down, Ben. I'm so tired I'm going right to bed. Give me a kiss."

They embraced and Ben slid across the seat and handed her down and watched her head for the brick walk that led to her house, then drove off. As she walked toward the porch Amy consciously began breathing deeply, trying to get the stuffy air of the hot ink-drenched newspaper office out of her lungs. It was then she picked up a new smell and halted. It was a smell of wood smoke.

That was curious, she thought. She and her father had eaten a quick supper at a café, so there had been no fire in the stove in their house that night. Her father, after helping load the papers on the buckboard, had walked home and Amy knew, from long custom, that he had gone directly to bed without bothering with a fire or coffee.

Now she looked over at the dark Bowers house, which was almost a match for their own house, since they had been built by the same carpenters. Had some of these drunken bounty hunters, noting the house was empty, broken in and were camping there? The gentle night breeze could only have brought it from the Bowers house since the wind direction was right and there were no other close neighbors.

The thought of this sneaky break-in infuriated her and now she stepped off the walk on to the hard-packed ground and headed for the Bowers' back porch. If she met any trouble, her calls would bring her father. As quietly as she could on this baked and stony ground she approached the house, halted, and listened. Inside she could hear voices, and her anger mounted still higher.

Mounting the steps of the back porch, she crossed it and knocked imperiously on the heavy door, calling, "Open up in there, whoever you are! Open up!" And she hammered on the door again.

The voices ceased and now she wondered, fear rising in her, what kind of bearded, drunken bounty hunter would answer.

When the door swung open, she could see nothing and she had her mouth open to scold when Tina said, "Why Amy. It's you, isn't it?"

"Tina! What in the world are you doing here? I thought the Kimballs hid you from the mob."

"They thought it would be cleverest for me to hide here and let the bounty hunters leave the country."

"Why didn't you tell me you were here?"

"There was nobody home at your place and I don't dare go out," Tina answered.

"Who were you talking to in there? Lew?"

Tina hesitated a moment and then said, "No. It's Cam Holgate."

Amy was stunned momentarily, and then she recovered herself. "What in the world is he doing here? Did he break in?"

There was a tone of anger and threat in Amy's voice that made Tina say hastily, "No, no. He didn't break in." She sighed. "It's a long story, Amy. Do you want to listen to it in the dark? Because I can't light a lamp for fear of the bounty hunters."

"I want to hear the story, but not here. Why don't you come over to my place? Cam Holgate, if you can hear me, you come too."

Arm in arm Tina and Amy went down the steps and headed for Amy's home. Cam, trailing, heard Amy say, "I'll make some coffee for us while you talk."

Both girls knew Amy's kitchen and they went in first and got a lamp lighted while Cam stood in the doorway. As Amy started the fire in the black kitchen stove, Tina looked at Cam. There was both a plea for help and a sensuous secretiveness in her eyes as she looked at him.

"Both of you sit down," Amy said. "This will take a while, but somebody get started." She looked directly at Cam and said, "You seem to turn up everywhere you're not wanted."

"I was invited here," Cam said dryly.

"Only to explain things. Sit down, both of you, while I get the coffee going."

A rectangular table, three chairs facing it, one at each end and one in the middle, stood against the left wall. Now Tina moved to the chair at the far end and Cam took the one at the near end, leaving the chair in the middle for Amy.

"Well, one of you start. I can hear you," Amy said.

Cam's head throbbed abominably and he was in no mood to answer Amy's questions which he was certain would be ferocious. He decided that since Tina had already proven to be an expert liar, he would let her tell her story and now he said, "You tell her, Tina."

"There's not really much to tell, Amy. Cam brought word to the ranch that the mob was on its way. When they came in sight, Cam gave me his horse and I circled north around that wild bunch. Lew and Abbie had already agreed the best place to hide would be my house because Ben had told the mob I was at the ranch and not at home."

"That makes a kind of left-handed sense," Amy said. "Go on."

"I left Cam's horse at the feed stable and sneaked down the back alleys till I got home. You weren't home, I could see. I waited till it was dark to cook my supper so nobody would see the smoke. Then Cam came. He wanted to check to see if I got here safely."

The coffeepot watered and put on the stove, Amy crossed to the table but instead of sitting down she put both hands on the back of the straight chair and looked first at Tina and then at Cam and it was to Cam she spoke. "All it should have taken was a knock on the door from you and an answer from Tina. What's going on here?"

"Ask Tina."

As Amy looked at Tina there was disapproval in her face and Tina flushed. Then Tina said, almost defiantly, "Amy, Cam and I are partners."

"Partners! In what?" Amy asked, scorn in her voice.

"We've thrown in together to try and find the escaped robber and the bullion and claim the reward."

Amy's full lips parted a little in disbelief. "Why, you're out of your mind, Tina. What do you know about this man?"

"Only that he helped me, and I still need help, Amy."

"That he can give you?" Amy asked sardonically.

"I think he can," Tina said stoutly. "You can see for yourself he's not one of these whiskey-drinking saddle tramps that want to bully me. Besides that, he was smart enough to come out and trade his warning about the mob for what I had seen of the two robbers. Working together, maybe I can identify the man that got away and Cam can make him tell us where the bullion is."

Now Amy turned her head to look at Cam and her amber eyes were speculative, but they held a touch of hostility still. "Very clever of you, Mr. Holgate."

"I think so too," Cam agreed.

"So what's Tina's share of the reward?"

"Tell her, Tina."

Tina said, "Ten percent."

Her glance still on Cam, Amy said, "None of this share-and-share-alike business, eh?"

"No," Cam said coldly. "I came here to get that reward money. I didn't come here to provide for Dan Bowers' widow for life."

"Well, you're honest about it anyway." To Tina Amy said, "You're a bad bargainer, Tina. But of course, it's your own business."

Cam looked from one girl to the other and privately assessed the differences between them. Both girls were beautiful, Tina, in her dark, wily way, Amy in her fair, forthright way. He wondered then if Amy had never seen the flaws in Tina. If she had, she had probably forgiven them. Sheriff Ben Judd had himself quite a girl in Amy, Cam thought—a better woman than he was a man, Cam guessed. In spite of her dislike of him, he admired those qualities in her that made her dislike him—her protectiveness of Tina, her skepticism of him, and her hard common sense.

Now Amy went over to the cupboard, brought out the cups, brought some milk from the cooler in the corner, and then brought the coffeepot over and poured their coffee.

Then Amy sat down, pulled up her chair and said, "How are you going to work with Cam, Tina? Are you going to hide in that house all day, eating cold food and meeting with Cam at night? Why don't you go back to Lew's?"

"That would mean Cam would have a six-mile ride every time he wanted to talk to me." To Cam, Tina said, "That's what you said, isn't it, Cam?"

At Cam's nod Amy said, "That's a pretty wretched existence you're forcing on her."

"Show me a better way we can be in touch with each other."

"I will." She turned to Tina. "Tina, we have that spare room upstairs and that's where you'll stay. If you think you're imposing on us, you're wrong. You can cook and keep the house and you'll have company three times a day. Cam can come and see you here whenever he wants. Now don't say 'No' because it makes too much sense."

"But will your father like that, Amy?"

"He'll love it. He loves you, you know it."

"Take up her offer, Tina," Cam said, "It's the only way you can beat the cabin fever you'll have over at your place."

Tina smiled and said, "It's kind of you, Amy, and I'll take up your offer."

"Good. As soon as we've finished coffee we'll go over and move some of your things."

"Can I help?" Cam said.

"You'd only be in the way," Amy said shortly.

Once their coffee was finished Cam stood up and said to Amy, "Thanks for everything." To Tina he said, "I don't know when I'll see you, Tina, but now I know where I can find you. Good night, ladies."

They bid him "Good night" and he left by the back door, circled the house, and was on the road. It had been a long day, he thought as he tramped up the dark rutted street, and he was bone weary. Still, in this one day he thought he was a little ahead of the rest of the bounty hunters. He had learned that the surviving robber's name was Wes Chance, that he was a squat two-hundred-plus-pounder of perhaps thirty-five, a sullen-faced bullyboy who was tough and daring. Now that he and Tina were partners there was no reason for her to hold back any information on Chance's whereabouts from him. Under questioning before Amy arrived at her place Tina had admitted that Chance had struck a match and had a look at him while he was knocked out. However, Tina had persuaded Chance not to get rid of him for fear of implicating both of them more deeply.

Too, Chance could not know of the bargain Tina had struck with him so that while Chance could recognize him he would still be afraid to move against him at this point. Chance had told Tina he was leaving, but for where?

Cam tried to put himself in Chance's place, he had roughly one hundred pounds of bullion hidden. Eventually Chance would have to move that bullion across the border into Mexico, for if he tried to dispose of it in this country he would become suspect immediately. He could, of course, sell it in small bits, but Cam reckoned he was not that patient a man. Moving it now, what with the country overrun with bounty hunters who examined every freight shipment and every wagon's cargo, would be extremely risky. The smart thing for Chance to do would be to wait until the bounty hunters were broke and gave up their roaming and searching and snooping and went home. After they had gone it would be safe and fairly easy to move the cargo of bullion across the border. Therefore it seemed reasonable that Chance would simply bide his time until this had blown over and the bounty hunters had gone. Cam reckoned there were at least a thousand old prospect holes in the hills where he could hide the bullion, and wait. So instead of searching those prospect holes, as many of the bounty hunters were doing, he must find Chance.

The wagon traffic from mine to mill was as heavy now as it had been during the day but the pedestrian traffic had tapered off. When he reached the lights of the business district he avoided that side of the street where the Cameo was and made his way beyond it before he started his cut across to his hotel. The Cameo, he noticed, was booming with business and as noisy or noisier than it had been at any time he passed it.

He halted, waiting for a high-wheeled ore wagon pulled by three teams of mules to pass him. There was a man upstreet who had been waiting to cross too and once the ore wagon was past him he moved through the cloud of dust it trailed and was gone. Cam waited until the dust had settled a bit and then crossed the road and reached the opposite boardwalk turning upstreet.

He was approaching an alley mouth now and just as he moved toward it he felt something ram into his back, it was unmistakably a gun and he halted.

"Turn in that alley up ahead," a voice said from behind him and the gun was jammed savagely into his back, putting him into motion. Remembering the man who had left the café at suppertime, Cam cursed himself for a fool. This would be one of Crowder's men, he knew. The evening's events had been so swift, violent, and absorbing, by turns, that he had forgotten Crowder entirely, and now he was paying for his forgetfulness.

A second man was waiting in the dark of the alley and he reached out and lifted Cam's gun from its holster.

"You took your time," the second man said.

Cam was about to answer when the other man said, "He took his."

They walked down this alley, turned right on a street and came to a low one-story adobe Mexican *fonda*. Crossing its patio they came to a door of a corner room which the men entered without knocking: each holding him by an arm, they propelled Cam into a big room.

The room they entered was much like a ranch bunkhouse. Double-deck bunks lined the walls and there was a big rectangular table with benches in the center of the room. A half-dozen men were seated on the benches playing poker under an overhead lamp around which moths and flies looped and buzzed. The room was stifling hot and smelled of tobacco and whiskey. There were several bottles on the table and one of them was in front of Crowder.

At their entrance, Crowder looked up and saw Cam and then lazily came to his feet. "Cash in your chips, gents. The game's over," he announced.

Standing, Crowder took a drink from the bottle before him, wiped his mouth on his sleeve, and then lazily counted his chips and got his money from the dealer. He was in no hurry, Cam thought, and wondered what lay in store for him. Had Crowder discovered the truth about Lew Kimball's well-intended lie that

Tina had left before Cam arrived? If he had he was in for trouble.

When all the players had cashed in their chips Crowder said pointedly, "Good night, you fellas. We'll get together again."

Three of the men rose and headed for the door, looking incuriously at Cam as they passed. The remaining men, Cam judged, were Crowder's crew, for they made no move to leave.

Now Crowder swung a leg over the bench, came around the table and halted at its end, then half sat on it, regarding Cam. Hatless now, his wild mop of pale hair seemed white under the lamplight. His dark face was flushed and Cam judged he had a skinful of whiskey, along with the other players at the table. They all looked at him as he stood between his two captors.

Crowder ran both thumbs under his belt, spat on the floor, and then said, "You ride a Hatchet-branded horse, Holgate?"

So they turned that up, Cam thought dismally. But how? "Yes."

"It's in the feed-stable corral down the street," Crowder said. "How did it get there?"

"Where else would I put him?"

"Hit him, Charlie," Crowder said.

Instantly, the guard on his right drove an arm across his own body and hit Cam in the jaw. The blow shoved him into the second guard, who pushed him away.

As Cam was shaking his head to clear it Crowder continued, "He was rode in here by a pretty woman, the hostler said. They claim Mrs. Bowers is mighty pretty. Kimball said you got to Diamond K after she left. What was she doing with your horse then?"

"Kimball lied. He wanted to help me."

Crowder pounced. "So you did talk to Mrs. Bowers."

"That's right."

"Well, now we've got the bark off," Crowder drawled. "What did you ask her and what did she tell you?"

"I asked her what all of us want to know, I reckon. What the bullion robber looked like."

"What did he?" Crowder demanded.

Cam only shook his head. "The sheriff's already told us. My size, about thirty, dressed like any of us."

"He got a name?"

"I reckon he had, but she didn't know it."

Crowder was silent a long moment watching Cam and then he said quietly, "Get up, boys, and circle him."

The crew got to their feet, moved over, passed Crowder and ringed Cam. When they were set Crowder continued, "You give Mrs. Bowers your horse for only that? I don't believe it. You already knew that. What else did she tell you?"

"Find her and ask her," Cam said bluntly. "If she left my horse at the feed stable, she must be here."

"We seen her house. It's dark and empty. What else did she tell you?"

"That's the lot of it," Cam said.

Again Crowder looked at him a long moment and then he said, "All right, boys. Go."

At Crowder's signal someone rammed into Cam's back, pitching him forward into a man who slugged out at his face. A second blow caught him on the side of the head and hurled him toward a third man who drove a fist in his belly. As he was bent over someone kicked him in the thigh, which staggered him into another man who chopped a blow at his cheek.

There was no defense against this number of men. Before he could get set for a blow he received one that threw him off balance. He struck out at bodies and faces that he couldn't hit and all the time he was taking punishment from all directions.

It was inevitable that a man should leap on his back and when he did Cam staggered under his weight, trying to protect his face with arms folded before his head. He took blows in the midriff and kicks in his legs that brought a pain his muscles and body could not accept. He fell forward on his face, the man on his back riding him down, and then he was kicked into oblivion.

He did not know how long he lay unconscious but when he moved and turned on his back Crowder was standing above him. He lay spread-eagled and now Crowder, looking down at him, said, "Ready for more? All you got to do is name a name."

"Name a name," Cam repeated from the bare edge of consciousness. He mumbled something through bruised lips and immediately Crowder dropped to one knee and bent over him.

"What'd you say? Say it again," Crowder said. "Can you hear me? Say it again."

What had he heard? Oh, a name. Now he mumbled, "Tim, Tim." He was silent a moment and then he said, "McCabe, Tim McCabe." After a pause, he said, his words slurred, "Used to be—hostler at feed stable."

Crowder rose saying, "Tim McCabe, used to be hostler at feed stable." He moved over to the table, picked up his hat, put it on, and said to the waiting men, "I'll go check that. I need some air."

The crew scattered around the table again and Cam lay on his back, arms outspread, waiting for the pain to subside and his senses to return. Presently, when he thought he had strength enough, he rolled over on his belly, drew his knees up under him, straightened up, put a hand on the table, and pulled himself unsteadily to his feet, head hung, nose bleeding.

The crew was seated again and drinking again, Cam noted, and now to test his legs, he pushed away from the table and began a slow uncertain circle. The crew paid him only scant attention and presently his mind began to function again. He knew he had to get out of here before Crowder returned with the news that no Tim McCabe had ever worked there. The beating would resume, he was certain.

The strength was slowly coming back into his legs but he shuffled around a second and wider circle as though he were still barely under control.

The end of his second circle brought him close to one of the crew seated on the bench and now he pretended to stagger and fall to his knees close to the man.

Still, the crew seemed to be paying no attention to him, talking among themselves about a return to the Cameo.

Gathering all his strength Cam lunged for the man's gun, got it, lifted it out of the holster, and then, hand on the bench, pushed himself to his feet. He brought the gun up, cocked, and now the crew, warned by a cry from a man across the table, came to their feet.

Cam backed off, the gun held before him, and the crew fell silent.

Finally one man across the table spoke, "If we all go for our guns at the same time, we'll get him. Go on three. One—"

Cam shot him in the leg and the man spun over the bench with a howl of pain and fell heavily to the floor.

"Go on. Draw," Cam taunted. "You're only dead once."

The crew remained motionless as Cam backed toward the door, opened it, stepped out into the night, closed the door, put a shot into the bolt hoping to wreck it, turned, and ran blindly out into the darkness.

In minutes he was lost in the maze of alleys and paths that ran between the miners' shacks. He could hear men calling to each other, but they were not close.

When the calling stopped, he got his bearings and made his way haltingly toward his hotel. When he reached it the patio was unlighted and he found his room, locked the door behind him, moved toward the bed, and fell face down on it.

In seconds he was in an exhausted sleep.

5

Like most of the other people in El Cuervo, Sheriff Ben Judd was an early riser. The cool of the early morning hours was the time to get work done. The blasting heat of midday was stupefying, the time to stay indoors and wait until the sun had heeled over before resuming work again.

The traffic of the ore wagons, which went on round the clock, was stirring up a little dust as the wagons went to and from the mines and mills. On his way to the feed stable to leave his horse Judd reined in before the tie rail of the Cameo. Stretched out on the hard-packed dirt walk under the Cameo's *portal* were a couple of dozen men lying there sleeping. While it was not unusual to spot a drunk or so asleep on the sidewalk when he came to work, Judd had never seen as many men there and he took this as a good omen. It meant that some of the bounty hunters had run out of money for shelter and that they would soon be on their way out of town. Maybe the bounty hunters were beginning to believe what he said that they had no chance of finding the vanished bullion and even less chance of finding the bullion robber.

He left his horse at the feed stable and then tramped back to the sheriff's office. Letting himself in with his key, he glanced at the floor, looking for the night marshal's report which was usually shoved under the door before the night marshal quit. There was no note this morning, which meant it had been a quiet night.

He crossed over to his battered rolltop desk, which was

jammed with the paper work he had not been able to get at since Jack Carpenter had invited the bounty hunters in.

Taking off his hat and shell belt and hanging them on the coatrack he sat down in the rickety swivel chair, rolled it up to the desk, and began to go through his long-neglected mail.

He was barely into it when he heard a knock on the doorframe and footsteps on the board floor behind him. Turning now, he saw Crowder, the loudmouthed bounty hunter who had already given him so much trouble.

Without being invited Crowder crossed the room and slacked into the barrel chair beside the desk. Shoving his hat on the back of his head, he said, "Morning, sheriff."

"Morning, Crowder," the sheriff said without enthusiasm.

"Had a little trouble over at my place last night. Thought you might want to hear about it."

"Where's your place?"

"A Mex place. They call it La Posada."

"And what kind of trouble."

"One of my men got shot."

"The night marshal never reported it. What happened?"

"Oh, it wasn't bad enough to report. Just a nick in the leg. Still, if it had been a foot higher he'd have one hell of a bellyache; he'd likely be dead."

"Well, what happened?"

"Remember this Cam Holgate? He's a bounty hunter too."

"I remember him," the sheriff said wryly.

"Well, we found out he got to Mrs. Bowers before we did, out at the Diamond K. He had a talk with her and we wanted to know what she told him. Damned if he didn't lie to us and while I was out checking up on his lie he pulled a gun and shot one of my men."

"Did you rough him up?"

"A little. Nothing serious. No call for shooting a man, however you look at it."

"What do you want out of me?"

Crowder's pale eyes widened in fake astonishment. "Brother, I don't know how it is in this-here town, but when you do that up in mountain country you get thrown in jail for shooting an unarmed man."

"Sure he was unarmed?"

"Me and five other fellas will swear to it."

"Yeah, I reckon you would. All right, I'll check into it."

"What's there to check?" Crowder demanded.

"I'll get his side of it."

"You ain't going to take his word against the six of us, are you?"

The sheriff snorted. "Come to that, I wouldn't take the word of the seven of you, but I said I'll check."

"What if he's got information the sheriff's office ought to have. Would you lock him up then?"

"That's for me to decide," the sheriff said flatly. "I said I'll check, and I will."

Crowder rose. "You keep him locked up a few days, sheriff, and you may find out something you want to know real bad."

"I heard you the first time. Now go over to the Cameo and hunt your gold, Crowder."

Crowder went out and now the sheriff tilted back in his chair, clasped his hands before him, and leaned his chin on locked fingers. Crowder's motive in reporting the shooting seemed plain enough. He hoped to talk the law into taking Holgate in and sweating out of him what Tina Bowers had told him. Yesterday when he called Crowder a barracks lawyer he was speaking the simple truth. Crowder hoped to use the sheriff to get the information he himself couldn't get from either Tina Bowers or Holgate. Still, he supposed a routine check-out of Holgate's story was in order.

Swearing softly to himself he put on his hat and shell belt, went out, locked the door behind him, and started the wearisome check of the dozen hotels and boardinghouses in the town.

The third hotel he checked had Cameron Holgate registered in room 12, which, the clerk said, opened up off the patio. The sheriff found the room and knocked peremptorily on the door.

A sleepy but savage voice from inside said, "Go away!"

"Open up, Holgate. This is Sheriff Judd."

Presently the door inched open and a gun barrel protruded through the crack, then it disappeared and the door swung open and the sheriff was facing Cam Holgate.

He was barely recognizable, the sheriff thought and he said, "Good God! What happened to you?"

"Come on in, sheriff," Holgate said through bruised lips. He turned and went inside the room and the sheriff followed.

"Take a chair," Cam said.

Judd moved over to the straight-back chair in front of the window and as he sat down he noticed the dried blood on the bed's coverlet and the imprint of a body lying diagonally across the bed. He had wakened Holgate, he was sure.

Now Cam stripped off his bloody shirt, moved over to the washstand, poured the basin full of water from the pitcher, and began to wash. His lean body, the sheriff noted, was one mass of contusions and bruises.

The sheriff waited while Cam gingerly washed his face; then Cam came erect and began gingerly to towel his face and neck, turning to the sheriff.

"Crowder?" the sheriff asked.

"Him and five others."

"He stopped by to see me this morning," Judd said. "He wants you arrested for shooting one of his men and for withholding information."

"Withholding it from him, you mean."

"From me too. He claims you found out something from Tina Bowers."

"Sure I talked with her out at Diamond K before that mob got there. I found out from her exactly what you found out." Cam shook his head. "She just didn't pay any attention to that pair, is all."

Now Cam went over to his blanket roll and he could not suppress a groan as he picked it up and tossed it on the bed. Unstrapping it, he unrolled blankets and brought out a clean cotton shirt.

As he was putting it on the sheriff asked, "What happened with Crowder last night?"

Cam told briefly of being kidnapped, disarmed, and taken to the big room of a Mexican hotel. He admitted to talking to Mrs. Bowers alone and then the action started. When he could give no more information than Crowder already had about the two robbers the whole bunch jumped him, beat him and kicked him, and knocked him unconscious. When he came to, Crowder promised more of the same if he didn't disclose the information Crowder wanted. Cam said he had lied about a onetime hostler, whose name he had made up, being connected with the robbery and Crowder left for the feed stable to check his story. It was then, Cam said, that he stole a gun from one of Crowder's drunken crew and braced them. When one of the crew invited all five to draw on him at the count of three Cam shot the man and escaped. He finished by saying, "If I'd waited for that three count, I'd have been a dead man, so I shot the man who was counting. I tried to hit him in the leg, but I don't know where I hit him."

"Right where you aimed," the sheriff said, and now he stood up. "I'd call that self-defense and justifiable, but I wonder if the next time it'll be self-defense."

"What does that mean?" Cam asked.

"They'll be hunting you. You going to hunt them?"

"Not any," Cam said. "I'll shoot if I'm shot at."

"Better have some other witnesses besides that crew. They'll lie you into jail, sure as you're born."

"Thanks, I'll remember that."

The sheriff started for the door and then halted and said, "I don't have to tell you to watch yourself."

Cam grinned crookedly and said, "No, you don't. I'm thinking of buying a hand mirror so I can watch who's coming up behind me."

The sheriff smiled and said, "Not a bad idea."

Out on the street the sheriff halted, looked across the street between the ore wagons, saw the doors of the *Times* open, and cut into the traffic.

When he entered the *Times* office Judd saw Amy sitting at the square desk; William Cross was back oiling a press under the light cast by the overhead kerosene lamp. Walking through the gate Judd came up to Amy, who had seen him come in, kissed her, and then slacked into William Cross's empty chair facing her.

"Still tired?" he asked.

"No, I had a good sleep when I finally got to bed."

"Just came from seeing your friend Holgate," Judd said.

Amy's eyebrows raised, "My friend? Hardly."

"He looks as if an ore wagon ran over him," Judd said. "He got in a fight with Crowder and his crew last night and got the hell whaled out of him. They like to made his face over, and his body's just one big bruise."

Amy frowned. "When I saw him last night he looked all right."

"When did you see him last night?"

Amy told him then what had happened after he had dropped her off and of Tina and Cam coming over to her house. She told him too of her invitation to Tina to stay in their spare room so that she would be less lonely and less at the mercy of the bounty hunters if they found her living in her house. She ended by telling him Tina's news. "Tina and Cam Holgate have thrown in together, Ben. They're going to try and find the killer and gold robber."

As was his habit when he was much disturbed Ben Judd tugged at his mustaches and there was anger in his eyes as he said, "That's the damnedest fool thing I ever heard of. Is Tina crazy?"

"She doesn't think so. Why? Is there anything wrong with it? Against the law, I mean?"

"No, but why is she doing it? What does she know about him?"

"She's doing it for a tenth of the reward money that he'll give her if he finds the killer and the gold."

Judd shook his head and said, "I don't like this, Amy. In the first place if she can spot that killer, she should come to me first. I'm the one who wants him for murder, and I come ahead of Jack Carpenter."

"Well, they'd probably turn him over to you. Or Carpenter would turn him over to you, wouldn't he?"

"That's not the same thing, and you know it. Tina has just plain turned bounty hunter."

"She could use the money, Ben."

Ben thought a moment and then asked sardonically, "What's she going to do? Ride all over the country with Holgate, looking for a man she likely doesn't remember?"

"Maybe if she sees him she will."

Ben rose now and started pacing the floor in a tight circle. "This Holgate is trouble, Amy, real trouble. He's likely to get killed. If she's with him she could get hurt, Amy."

"Why do you say he's likely to get killed?"

"First, he gunned down one of Crowder's crew. They'll want to get even. Second, they think he's got an inside track to Tina. Come to that, he has. Third, if they think he's getting close to that gold they'll get him out of the way."

"Does Holgate know all this?"

"I warned him."

"But what are you doing about all this, Ben?"

Judd halted and looked at her. "What can I do, Amy? Jack Carpenter's big reward has invited every vulture in the Southwest to this town. With that kind of money at stake they won't stop at murder or bushwhacking. If they got really ornery they'd tear up this town. There's only me and the night marshal to stop them."

"Couldn't you deputize enough men and run them out?"

The sheriff shook his head. "They've got a right to be here. Besides, the saloons and stores are all making money out of them." Then he added bitterly, "Damn that Jack Carpenter, anyway."

6

During the breakfast, which was slow going because of his bruised lips and face, Cam had a chance to go over what Tina had told him last night about Wes Chance. He had a horse lot at the south edge of town and from here he traded and swapped horses and supplied the mines with mules when he could get them. Tina had said Chance told her he was leaving town but that could have been a lie, Cam judged. He probably wanted her off his back. The best way to do it would be to say he wouldn't be here.

Finished with breakfast he hit the street, heading for the feed stable and his horse. Although he did not know the names of Crowder's crew he thought he could recognize them in time to be on his guard. Nothing happened on the way to the stable and once he was there he saw that nobody was waiting for him. His horse saddled, he mounted and moved a block away from Main Street to get out of the dust of the wagon traffic and then turned south.

It wasn't hard to pick up Chance's place of business on the edge of town. It consisted of a very large corral made of stout posts and crossbars. Along the far side was a long open-faced shed which provided shade for the horses. There were about twenty horses in the corral and three men were breaking a horse while two other men squatted in the shade and watched. As far as Cam could tell these were all Mexican hands and watching them handle the unbroken horse he could see they were both rough and expert.

A one-story adobe building squatted by the big gate and had an entrance both on the street and from the corral.

Cam rode up to this building. The door was open, and he dismounted, tied his horse to the worn tie rail in front of the door, and then tramped across the hard-packed adobe and stepped through the doorway.

Two men ceased their talking at his entrance and as his eyes adjusted to the darkness of the room, Cam saw with a shock of surprise and excitement that the man seated at the desk answered Tina's description of Wes Chance. Chance had been talking to an older white-haired man dressed in worn and filthy range clothes and it was to this man that Cam addressed himself.

"You Mr. Wes Chance."

The older man flicked a thumb at Chance and said, "That's him."

Cam looked at Chance now and knew that in spite of his bruised face Chance recognized him. Chance was a stocky man dressed in range clothes and almost no neck separated his heavy head from his thick shoulders. His mustaches were black as was his thick coarse hair, but his heavy face had a sullenness about it that was faintly sinister. Chance could not entirely hide the surprise in his dark eyes at Cam's appearance, for he had not looked this way when Chance had seen him last night.

"What can I do for you?" Chance said. His voice was deep and pleasant enough, Cam thought.

"They tell me you're a horse trader, Chance. That right?"

"That's my business."

"Well I want to sell my horse and maybe buy another one. Want to take a look at him?"

Chance rose slowly and said, "What's the matter with him?"

"Nothing. I just need some money." He raised a hand to his face and said, "I got jumped in an alley last night. Three men, they beat me up and cleaned me out."

Chance came closer, stopped, tilted his head and looked at Cam's face.

"They didn't have to do that, did they?"

"All I know is that they did."

Chance moved past him and went outside, Cam trailing him, the third man trailing Cam.

Once out in the harsh sunlight Chance circled Cam's dun, moved up, opened the horse's jaws to look at his teeth, and then felt pasterns and hocks. He backed up, took another look from ten feet off, and then said, "Twenty dollars."

"Did you say fifty?" Cam said.

Chance's mustache lifted in a faint grin and he said, "Hell, he's worth fifty, but I said twenty. That's too much horse for this country." He gestured loosely toward the corral, "That stuff is good enough for us."

Cam turned, went over to the gate, leaned on the top cross-bar, and took a look at the horse inside. Chance trailed up behind him and joined him. Here beside him, Cam thought, was the man he had come to hunt, all hundred and fifty thousand dollars' worth of him, but without the bullion he was just another man. To be sure he was a killer, maybe a twice-over killer, but his arrest and conviction came last in order of importance.

"I see what you mean," Cam said. "They're a pretty sore lot."

"That they are," Chance agreed.

Both men were silent. Looking at the horses that were nuzzling around the bordered-off hay under the shed roof.

"Half of them ain't broke to either saddle or harness," Chance said. "Them damn Injuns across the border will catch them or walk 'em down and sell 'em to us. We drive 'em up and break 'em but it's mostly mules we're after for the mines."

Pretending to regard the horses, Cam looked at the buildings behind the office. There was a row of adobe buildings with children playing out on the hard-packed dirt, women watching, and he supposed these were the wives and children of the men Chance employed. There was a rickety blacksmith's shop, a garden patch beyond it, and that was all. In theory Chance could have brought in the bullion and hidden it on this place, but Cam doubted that he had. With children and hired hands and their families around, there was too much risk of someone accidentally stumbling on it. It was much safer to hide it in the vast desert that stretched all around them.

Cam pushed away from the gate now and said, "Well, I don't reckon we do business, Chance. I don't want what you got and you can't afford what I got."

Chance looked at Cam's horse again and said, "I might go ten higher."

"You should."

"Only after I check his wind. Mind if I run him?"

"He's practically your horse. Go ahead."

Chance went over to the dun, untied him, mounted, put him out in the road, then lifted him into a trot and then a gallop. Cam smiled faintly. His ruse was succeeding. If the dun's wind was sound, and it was, Chance would buy him. And Cam was sure that once he had bought him he would not sell him, but keep him for his own. The dun was that kind of horse—tough, fast, a stayer, gentle and easy gaited.

But what Chance did not know yet was that the heel calks on the dun's left hind shoe were longer than average to counter a tendency to walk on the heel of that hoof. The shoe left a distinctive deep print unlike any other, and a man who knew what to look for could easily track the dun from horseback.

Chance came back at a gallop, reined in, dismounted, and listened. The dun was breathing hard but there was no give-away whistle or coughing.

"That's a hell of a horse. He's worth more than I'm paying," Chance said.

"I know that," Cam said. "Let's go pick me out a horse."

The choice didn't take long. Cam picked out a rangy bay that was saddle broken. After the dun was turned in and the bay saddled, Cam and Chance exchanged bills of sale. Cam received his money, and rode off.

Cam wondered what Chance was thinking. Surely Chance would associate him with Tina, but would he be interested enough to go to Tina and question her? Cam doubted it. Chance would reason the threat he and Tina held over each other was too binding to trifle or trade with. Cam also thought that his own appearance at Chance's was reasonable enough. If a man was beat up and robbed he only had his horse, his saddle, and his gun left him and the sale of the horse would get him eating money for a while.

Cam took a roundabout way back to the feed stable, left his horse, and took another roundabout way which brought him down the alley behind Amy's house.

He knocked on the back door and presently Tina opened it and saw him. She looked at his bruised face and gave a small cry of dismay. Taking his arm she drew him into the kitchen.

Closing the door she looked at him more closely and then whispered, "Oh, you poor darling," moved up to him, and put her arms around him. She kissed his lips and face ever so gently, moving her body against his. He could see the green dress she was wearing under a full apron but he could have sworn she had nothing on under that dress.

Gently he disengaged her arms, saying, "I thought our bargain was already sealed."

She ignored his comment and said, "Cam, what happened?"

Cam began briefly to tell her what had happened after he left them last night. As he was talking Tina guided him to one of the chairs at the kitchen table; he might have been an aging cripple from the way she steered him to the chair. She sat down now in the chair opposite him and listened in rapt silence as he told her of his escape and of Sheriff Judd's visit this morning prompted by Crowder's visit to the sheriff.

When he was finished, Tina said, "But they didn't get anything about us from you, did they?" When Cam said, "No," a look of immense relief came over her lovely face.

Now Tina rose, moved over to the cupboard and got down two coffee cups, poured the coffee at the stove, and brought the cups over to the table. While she was doing this she told about Lew Kimball's visit to her this morning. She had seen him try the front and back doors of her house before she called him over. Lew had agreed that she had been wise to move in with Amy. Tina said she shooed him away before his horse could be recognized and somebody would get curious about why he was calling at this house.

Cam waited impatiently until she was finished and then he said, "I talked with Wes Chance this morning, Tina."

A look of fear crossed Tina's face and she asked, "Did he recognize you?"

"I'm sure he did, but then I had a good reason to go out there." Cam then told her of his lie to Chance that he had been beaten up and robbed and of having to sell his horse for money to live on. It was a natural move for any broke cowhand, Cam said, and the marks on his face backed up the story of his beating. Cam finished by saying, "At least I know who I'm looking for now."

"What do we do now, Cam?"

"Nothing to him until he leads us to the gold." He paused and shook his head. "We've got to move him out of there, Tina, some way. He can sit on that money until all of us have forgotten about it unless we move him to the gold. I think I've got a way to do it."

Tina said nothing, waiting.

Cam said, "Suppose you got a letter in the mail, Tina, from a man you've never heard of. He says he's been looking for you at the Diamond K and at your house and he can't find you. He says he was on the train the night of the murders. He thinks he saw the missing robber and he followed him to his house but he's not sure he's the man. He says you were sitting a lot closer to the robber than he was. He asks if you'll let him pick you up —you name the place—and go with him to see the man he thinks is the robber. If you think so too then you both go to Jack Carpenter and the sheriff with your story. He says he knows both of you can't claim the reward because you haven't found the bullion but he thinks Jack Carpenter would be so glad to find his son's killer that he would come up with some kind of reward you could split."

Tina frowned. "What do I do with this letter and who writes it?"

"I write it," Cam said. "I'll mail it and Amy can bring it

home to you. You open it, then scribble a note to Wes Chance. Put your note and the letter in an envelope and address it to Chance. Your note should say that the letter came in your mail and you have to answer it because if you don't this man might go to the sheriff alone. Tell him that to save both your necks he'd better get out of town."

"Why don't you say in your letter that he wants to take both me and the sheriff to identify this man and arrest him?"

"Good idea," Cam said. "Oh, write Wes that you won't answer this man's letter until you hear from him that he's gone."

"What do you think Wes will do, Cam?"

"I know what I'd do if I were in Chance's place. I'd take a cold look at it. I'd figure that this fellow would go to the sheriff even if you didn't help him in the identification. That would bring the sheriff down on me for questioning. In other words I'd figure I'd worn out this town and I'd pick up the gold, head for Mexico, and stay away from here."

Tina nodded and then said, "Let me hunt up some paper."

While Tina was in the other room searching for writing materials, Cam composed the letter in his mind. It shouldn't be the illiterate scribble of an impetuous man but rather the writing of a man of mature and seasoned judgment.

Tina returned with pen and ink and Cam, with Tina watching over his shoulder, slowly wrote the letter. When he was finished he handed it to Tina and watched her read it.

When she had done so she put the paper down and Cam noticed she was frowning. "Anything wrong?" he asked.

"You said this is meant to get Wes on the move, didn't you?" At Cam's nod she went on, "If he does get on the move, how do you follow him? He'll see you and probably wait for you and shoot you."

Cam then told her of the special shoes on the hind feet of the dun he had sold Chance. It would be easy to track him once his direction of travel was established, Cam said. It wouldn't be necessary to keep Chance in sight at all.

Tina seemed satisfied with his explanation and now Cam folded the letter, signed the name Tom Yates to it, and put it in the envelope and addressed it to Mrs. Dan Bowers, El Cuervo. He rose then, put the letter in his pocket and said, "You're sure Amy will pick this up?"

"The last thing she said when she left the house this morning was that she'd pick up my mail. Yes, I'm sure."

"This should be in your mail before noon. Don't show it to Amy. After she's gone back to work I'll stop by here and pick up the letter with your note in it."

Tina nodded and moved up to him. "Till this afternoon," she said and held up her face to be kissed.

Cam kissed her gently and moved away before she could put her body against his.

Tramping back to the post office, which was in a corner of Johnson's General Store, Cam thought about Tina and her affectionate way with him. It was obvious she was throwing herself at him and the reason for it wasn't hard to guess. She was desirable and she knew it. If she could get any hold on his affections, make him love her, even a little, her chances of getting a bigger share of the reward money were increased. If she could tease him into making love to her she would have a powerful hold on him. The trouble was, Cam thought, she was a very desirable woman but as dangerous as a rattler.

7

Amy saved her news until she and her father and Tina had eaten the noon meal that Tina had prepared. Tina had received a couple of consolation notes from distant relatives and friends in this morning's mail and she was commenting soberly on them as Amy poured the coffee, returned the pot to the stove, and sat down.

When Tina was finished and William Cross had made appropriate comments on how slowly news traveled to the outside world from this part of the country, Amy said, "Your partner got in some trouble after he left us last night, Tina."

"Doesn't he look dreadful?" Tina asked.

Amy looked curiously at her. "Do you mean he's been here?"

"Yes, he stopped by. He told me he had to sell his horse to get money to eat on."

"Then you know about his fight with Crowder and his crew?" At Tina's nod, Amy went on, saying, "Ben's pretty unhappy about your teaming up with Holgate. Ben's afraid for your safety, Tina."

"Ben's right, too," William Cross said. "Holgate seems to be in nothing but trouble since he rode into town."

"Not trouble he's made. It's trouble he's trying to avoid," Tina said warmly.

"It's trouble whoever makes it," William Cross said. He moved his coffee cup out of the way, folded his arms, and regarded Tina fondly. "For the life of me I can't see how you and Holgate can team up and get any results. You're in hiding and can't be seen on the streets. He's fighting this roughneck crew of Crowder's. How do you two intend to work together?"

"Why, if he sees a man that answers the description I gave of the robber, he'll have me identify him. I suppose we could do that after dark, couldn't we?"

"As a thousand-to-one shot, maybe," William Cross said. "The only other way you could help him would be for you both to hire a buggy, get a black veil for yourself, and drive up and down the streets of this town day after day. You'd only have to make a couple of patrols of the town before everybody knew who he was and who you were. Whoever you're looking for would simply leave town."

Amy said, "Besides that, you'd be sitting next to Holgate when Crowder's men jump him."

"What do you think I should do?" Tina asked.

William Cross took a sip of his coffee, set the cup gently down in the saucer, and said, "First, be sensible. I like this Holgate's spunk, but he's using you, Tina. He could very easily get you hurt. If they're watching him, sooner or later they'll see him come in here and wonder why. All it takes is for you to answer a knock on the door and then you're in that same mess again."

Amy said now, "Tina, the thing for you to do is stop seeing him. Tell him you've changed your mind. Once these bounty hunters are gone and you can move around town, you can still be on the lookout for the man you think is the robber. If you spot him, go to Ben and let him handle it from there on in."

"But can Ben find the money?" Tina asked.

"Can Holgate?" Amy countered.

"I think he can," Tina said stoutly. "Ben's got a job. Cam hasn't. He's working full time on it and Ben can't."

"But Ben's got the law on his side," Amy said.

"Maybe that's a hindrance," Tina said pointedly. "Could he have stopped those toughs from coming out to Lew's to hunt me down?"

"He didn't know they were going out there," Amy said, almost angrily.

"But Cam Holgate did," Tina pointed out. "You both know I like Ben, but I'm just one of a dozen troubles that he has to look after. He's after the killer. Cam Holgate is after both the killer and the gold."

"But Ben's after both the killer and the gold too. He has to be."

Tina shook her head. "It's not the same, Amy. Ben's kind and easygoing, the right man in the right job. Cam's a different kind of man. He's quick and rough and reckless. I think he's what I need if I'm ever to get any part of Jack Carpenter's reward."

"Even if you risk your life in getting it?" Amy asked.

William Cross put in gently, "It's her choice, Amy, not yours."

"So it is," Amy said shortly. She rose and began to clear the table with Tina helping her. There was a new hardness about Tina that surprised her. No, not hardness, perhaps firmness would be a better description. She could not find it in her heart to blame Tina for wanting a share of the reward money if the bullion was ever found. After all, her husband had died trying to save it and had left her with little or nothing except their house and some clothes. Perhaps Tina was right to gamble on this hardfisted brawler rather than to wait for justice—a sometimes blind justice—to take its course.

Beyond that, however, she could not help feeling a small resentment at Tina's comparison of Ben and Cam Holgate. While Tina had taken nothing from Ben, she had added something to Holgate's stature and Amy wondered if something was lacking in her own perception. While Holgate had more than his share of brashness and energy she wondered about the character of the man beyond these qualities. He was frank to bluntness and unashamed of what he was and what he was doing.

8

When Cam reckoned that Amy and her father had gone back to the newspaper office he again sought the alley behind the Cross house, went up to the open back door, and knocked on the doorframe.

Tina, from her seat at the kitchen table, called, "Come in, Cam. I'm just addressing the envelope. Sit down." She pointed with a pen to a paper on the table and said, "Want to read my note to Wes?"

Cam came over and, still standing, picked up Tina's note and read it. In a bold, almost unfeminine hand, she had written everything Cam told her to write. She had underlined that part of her message saying that she would do nothing until she heard from him as to when he was leaving town.

Handing it back to her and watching her fold it, Cam asked, "Do you think he'll answer by messenger or write?"

"I think he'll write," Tina said. "Even if he could find me I don't think he'd trust a messenger."

"How soon?"

"Well, how soon would you if you were in his boots?"

"Right away," Cam said. "I'll drop by around this time tomorrow when the Crosses are gone and see if you've got an answer."

Tina nodded, rose, and gave him the letter, which he put in his hip pocket. He turned then, heading for the door, but Tina cut him off. Again she put her arms around him and lifted her face for a kiss. Her lips were warm and moist and tantalizing and Cam gently disengaged her arms and said with a smile, "The doctor says the ration is no more than two a day, Tina."

She smiled knowingly and Cam moved past her out into the blasting sunlight.

On his way up the dusty road Tina was still in his mind, the taste of her on his lips. Each time they'd met she'd become more brazen, even wanton, and Cam knew she was planning this with all her woman's cunning. At each of their meetings she would become more forward and now Cam voiced a silent hope that Wes Chance's answer would come soon so that he could get away from this woman.

As he moved up toward the Cameo he could hear the din of the bounty hunters inside and it reminded him to be on the alert for Crowder and his gang. He supposed the bounty hunters roamed the countryside in the early morning and late evening, but in the middle of the day they all seemed to jam the Cameo.

Crossing the dusty street to Johnson's and the post office, Cam felt a deep weariness. Last night's beating was catching up with him, he supposed. Tramping into the store he moved toward the rear to the boarded-up cubicle that was the El Cuervo post office. He put his letter in the mail slot and headed for the street. His head was throbbing, his muscles aching, and he knew what he was going to do. The bed in his hotel room was calling as no bed had ever called before.

In the lobby, he started for the desk, then remembered he had not locked his door, since there was nothing worth stealing in his room. He made for the patio door. Just outside the door from the lobby a Mexican was watering down the flagstones and sweeping them. Cam spoke to him and received a nod and a smile in reply. Reaching his room door, Cam palmed the door open took a step inside and abruptly halted. Silhouetted against the drawn curtains of the window across the darkened room was the figure of a man standing. Although it was almost dark in the room, Cam could make out another figure just rising from the bed.

Now the man at the window moved and Cam saw his right

69

arm drive down as if for his gun. Instinctively Cam took a step backward to put the door between himself and the man on the bed and at the same time streaked his hand toward his own gun. Cocking it the second his hand touched the gun butt, he lifted the gun just clear of the holster, tilted it, and shot at the man against the curtains.

He heard the grunt of driven breath from the man and then Cam wheeled, stepped outside, rounded the doorframe, flattened himself against the wall, and only then heard the man fall.

Cam called sharply, "Come out of there with your hands over your head."

"Coming," a voice said. And Cam recognized it as the voice of Crowder.

Inside the room Crowder moved swiftly to his downed companion, yanked the gun from his holster, took out his own gun, moved to the curtained window, parted the curtains, and looked out and up at the roof of the building adjoining. It was a one-story adobe separated from the hotel by a four-foot-wide weedy walkway. Swiftly, surely, then Crowder pitched one gun up on the flat roof of the building. The second gun followed in an accurate arc.

"Hurry it," Cam called.

The guns disposed of, Crowder raised his hands over his head and walked out of the door.

When he and Cam faced each other and Cam had his look he said, "All right, put your hands down."

Crowder lowered his hands and said angrily, "I looked at Ed, I think you killed him."

"He was going for his gun."

"He didn't have a gun," Crowder said still angrily. "I don't have a gun either."

"Why not?"

"Because you're so goddamned hot-tempered! We left our guns in our room. We only wanted to talk to you."

"Stay right here," Cam said and then he moved into the room. Ed had fallen on his face and now Cam turned him over and saw that the slug from his gun had caught Ed in the chest. He was, as Crowder said, dead, very dead. Now Cam opened the curtains to throw more light into the room and then began his search for the two men's guns. There wasn't much of any place to hide them. They weren't under the bed and they weren't in the drawers of the dresser, nor were they under the blankets of the bed.

Crowder was standing in the same spot when Cam came out. Cam halted beside him and said grimly, "He's dead, all right."

Now Cam looked about him. A half-dozen men were gathered in front of the lobby entrance to the patio, curious but careful. The Mexican sweeper, who had seen every move in this, was standing motionless, watching.

Now Cam said, "What were you doing in my room?"

"I told you. Waiting to talk to you."

"How'd you get in?"

"Through the window."

"Why didn't you wait in the lobby?"

"It was too damned hot. Besides we wanted to talk to you alone. After last night we knew you wouldn't come to our room so we came to yours."

At that moment Sheriff Ben Judd came through the lobby door at a jog, shouldered through the few onlookers, and came more slowly up to them.

"What was the shot?" the sheriff asked. "It came from this building."

"I shot," Cam said calmly. "I killed a man. He's in my room."

The sheriff looked at Cam with a grim distaste and said, "Stay here, both of you," then walked into Cam's room. After confirming the man on the floor was dead he came out and halted before Cam and Crowder. "All right. What's the story?" the sheriff asked. "Holgate first."

Cam told of opening his door and seeing the figure of a man silhouetted against the curtains of the darkened room and also of seeing another man sitting on the bed. The man silhouetted against the curtains went for his gun, Cam said, and Cam simply beat him to the draw.

"That's a damn lie," Crowder said flatly. "I was the man on the bed and Ed was the man standing. Neither one of us had a gun, and that was on purpose. We figured if he saw we didn't have guns and he did have one he'd talk with us."

Judd said to Cam, "Did you say anything when you saw these two men?"

"Nobody said a word. They didn't and I didn't."

"Couldn't you see he didn't have a gun?" the sheriff asked.

"No. The curtains were pulled. It was dark. I saw his arm move and I figured he was going for his gun."

"You saw his arm move," Judd said sardonically. "Saw the arm of a person move, so you shot. What if you'd shot the cleaning woman?"

"The cleaning woman don't wear hats," Cam said dryly.

Judd gave him a sour look and then turned his attention to Crowder. "What's your story. What were you doing in the room?"

Crowder told the same story he had told Cam—wanting out of the heat, wanting privacy for their talk with Cam, he and Ed had left their guns in their room and climbed through the window of Cam's room. Sure they were trespassing, Crowder admitted. But it was a harmless kind of trespassing especially since they weren't armed. All they wanted was a peaceable talk with Holgate to make a deal with him if they could about what Mrs. Bowers had told him, so what better place to wait for him than in his room? They were simply waiting when he hurtled in and shot Ed on sight. Crowder finished by saying, "I can understand a man being a little surprised to find a stranger in his room but to kill him on sight don't make sense. Why didn't he ask our names and what we wanted? If he didn't like us being there why didn't he call the owner and have us thrown out?"

The sheriff nodded and then addressed Cam. "Did anybody see this besides you and Crowder?"

"That Mexican yardman," Cam said, pointing to the attentive, still motionless sweeper.

The sheriff turned, called, *"Oiga!"* and beckoned, and the houseman moved over to join them.

In swift Spanish, Judd began to question him and the answers came in Spanish. The sweeper talked at length and finally Judd nodded, then looked at Cam and said, "He says you opened the door, took a step in, drew your gun and shot, then backed out, hid against the wall, and called Crowder out. That's all he knows."

"That's all he saw," Cam said.

The sheriff frowned and shook his head. "What was so valuable in that room that you'd shoot an unarmed man to protect it?"

"Me," Cam said flatly.

Again Cam saw the swift flash of anger in the sheriff's eyes. Now the sheriff held out his hand and said, "Give me your gun, Holgate?"

"Am I under arrest?"

"I said, give me your gun."

The two men looked at each other steadily and the sheriff still held out his hand. Then Cam shrugged, lifted his gun from its holster, and tendered it to the sheriff, saying, "You didn't answer my question."

The sheriff took the gun, rammed it in his waistband, and said, "Yes, you're under arrest." He tilted his head toward the door. "There's an unarmed dead man in there that you shot on sight. You never asked him who he was or why he was there. You just killed him. From here on in it's up to the district attorney to decide whether to prosecute or not."

"Can I get bail?"

"Murder isn't a bailable offense," the sheriff said flatly. "Now come along." Judd looked at Crowder now. "You show up at J.P. Court tonight in Johnson's back room across the street. At eight o'clock, Crowder. If you aren't there I'll come and get you. Do you want that in writing? The summons, I mean."

"I'll be there," Crowder said. "What will the charge be?"

"Unlawful entering. You'll be fined if you plead guilty and you'd be smart to, since you've already told me that you did."

As Cam and the sheriff headed for the lobby door Cam said, "How long will this business take, sheriff?"

"Hard to tell. The district attorney's in San Isbel. He'll be there three or four more days."

"And I wait for him in jail?"

"That's what the book says," the sheriff said.

In the sheriff's office Cam was asked to empty his pockets on the desk and the contents were put in a canvas sack by the sheriff and locked in his desk drawer. Afterward the sheriff took down a ring of large keys hanging from a nail in the wall above his desk, took one of them, moved over to the door of the cellblock, swung it open, stepped aside, and motioned for Cam to enter. He moved into a six-cell cellblock, three cells on either side of the walkway. The heat was so savagely intense in this room that Cam halted and opened his mouth to get enough air.

Stepping around him, the sheriff put a key in the middle cell of the left bank and as he swung the barred door open, he said, "This is the hottest part of the day. I'll leave that office door open and it'll cool off a little."

"You couldn't keep a horse or a dog in a place like this. They'd die," Cam said.

"Oh, not if they had enough water. I'll go and get yours. Now step inside."

Cam stepped into the cell and the sheriff locked the door behind him and then left the cellblock.

His head was pounding, his body bone weary, Cam looked at the bleak cell that was to be his home until the district attorney returned. It held only a blanket-covered cot with an upended bucket resting on a newspaper on the floor at the foot of it. As he moved over to the cot Cam peeled off his sweat-wet shirt, threw it on the blanket, sat down, and was pulling off his boots when the sheriff returned.

Judd was carrying a large canvas-covered canteen which was dripping water. Shoving the canteen through the bars, he set it on the floor, then straightened up and said, "If you put the canteen in the window it'll keep the water a little cooler." He looked at Cam thoughtfully and tugged absently at his mustache. "Anything you want to tell me you didn't say over there?"

"No. I just want to repeat something," Cam said wearily. "I honestly thought I was about to get gunned down."

Judd shook his head. "They had a chance to gun you down last night and didn't. Why would they gun you down today?"

"Because I shot one of Crowder's men last night."

"No. You're no good to them dead. I believe they only wanted to talk to you like they said. Still it's up to the district attorney to make the charge or drop it. All I can do is hold you for him."

"Well, you're doing it," Cam said sourly.

"I'm going out to take care of the dead man, Holgate. I'll have to lock the street door but the windows in my office are open. That's the coolest I can make it for you."

He went out and now Cam pulled off his other boot and stretched out on the cot, using his wet shirt for a pillow.

He was, he thought with a gray distaste for himself, in one hell of a bind. Just when light was beginning to show at the end of the tunnel he was traveling he'd pulled the roof down on himself. If he had to stay in this hellhole of a jail for five more days it meant that Wes Chance, spooked by the letter and Tina's note, would have most of a week in which to pick up the gold and head the short distance to the border and Mexico.

Given even a slight wind during those five days Chance's tracks would be obliterated. Even if the district attorney decided not to press charges and freed him it would be too late.

All his planning and scheming had amounted to nothing in the end. If he'd had his wits about him when he opened the door to his room he would have thought of just those factors the sheriff had pointed out—he had nothing of value in the room and if Crowder was waiting for him Crowder would not kill him, since he hadn't killed him the night before. Had the unconscious fear of another beating like he got last night driven him to his quick but wrong decision? Perhaps. A more likely explanation was that he was so exhausted and beaten that he didn't even stop to think. His reaction was instinctive and wrong, of course. He was going back over the whole thing again when blessed sleep came to him.

It was thirst that wakened him and he lay there panting, his mouth open and dry from the savage heat. Suddenly he remembered the canteen that he had forgotten to put in the window to catch whatever breeze came through. Rising painfully he got to his feet and moved over to the canteen where the sheriff had left it on the floor. He drank deeply from it and only when his thirst was quenched was he conscious of voices in the sheriff's office. One was that of a woman and it held a strange tight anger, although he could not make out what she was saying. Judd's answers were argumentative, although again he could not make out what Judd was saying.

It really didn't interest him. He lifted the canteen over his head now and doused his head and face with the lukewarm water; afterward, the water already cooling his sweating body, he took the canteen over to the window and wedged it between the high bars and looked at the sky, trying to gauge the time of day and how long he had slept.

His back was to the walkway when he heard a woman's voice exclaim, "Heavens, Ben! How can you keep a human being locked in this oven?"

Cam turned and saw Amy Cross staring at him, the sheriff behind her.

"Ask the commissioners. They built the jail. I only run it," Judd said sullenly.

Amy did not answer. She was looking at Cam and at his bruised and beaten body, her mouth open a little in surprise.

"Your first visitor, Holgate." To Amy, Judd said, "Want me to lock you in so you can sit down, Amy?"

"Yes." And then she added, "Leave us alone and close the door."

As he unlocked the door the sheriff said, "It'll be twice as hot if I close it."

"But close it anyway," Amy said.

Judd opened the door and Amy walked into the cell. Cam could see the beads of perspiration already forming on her upper lip and forehead. She walked over to the cot and sat down and waited until Judd had closed the door into the office.

Then she looked at Cam's bruised body and shook her head. "Don't those bruises hurt, Cam?" she asked.

Cam nodded. "They yell at me once in a while to remind me they're there."

Amy smiled woodenly and then tucked back a strand of hair and Cam was only then aware of her uneasiness. He did not try to help her but remained standing, watching her. Finally she raised her glance to him and said, "I've got Ben's story for the *Times*, Cam. Will you give me yours?"

"They've got to be the same, don't they?"

"That's what I want to find out. That's why I sent Ben out. And please sit down. You look exhausted."

He was, and now he sat down at the foot of the cot. He was aware that he stank of sweat and knew she was aware too, but there was nothing to do about it.

Beginning with his greeting to the yardman as he stepped out of the lobby on his way to his room, he told of opening the door of his darkened room.

"Hold on, Cam," Amy interrupted. "Did you pull those curtains before you left your room?"

"No." He thought a moment. "Maybe the cleaning woman did it to keep the heat out. Or maybe Crowder did it to get me into the room before I could see them."

Amy nodded and said, "Go on."

Cam then described seeing the figure framed in front of the curtained window and the man on the bed, and of his conviction that the man at the window was going for his gun. His own draw had been fast, the shot accurate. As fast as he could, he backed out and flattened himself against the wall, calling Crowder out. On Crowder's surrender and statement that he was unarmed as well as his companion, Cam had searched the room for their guns and couldn't find them. That was when Ben Judd took over and he too searched the room, came to his conclusion, and arrested him, Cam finished.

Amy, her face shining with perspiration, heard him out. When he was finished she said, "Cam, have you ever been to a dance or a political meeting where the men are asked to check their guns?"

"Lots of times."

"How did you do it?"

"Why, I took off my shell belt and—" He stopped in midsentence, seeing what she was driving at. "I get it."

"Exactly. If they truly left their guns in their rooms they wouldn't have been wearing shell belts, would they?" Her fisted hand came down on her knee. "They had guns, Cam! And Crowder got rid of them."

Cam rubbed his sweating face with both hands, silently cursing his own stupidity. He'd been too tired and too concerned over killing a man to think it strange Crowder and his gunhand were wearing shell belts.

His hands dropped and he looked at Amy. Perspiration was staining her blue dress wherever it touched her skin.

"Did you tell Ben that?"

"Yes." She hesitated. "He didn't agree. We—we quarreled, but I made him look in that weed patch between the two buildings outside your window. He didn't find the guns, of course."

"All Crowder had to do was wait until we left for here, then pick up the guns," Cam said softly, bitterly.

"That's what I told Ben." She was silent a moment, thinking. "Cam, after you shot and backed out of the room, you couldn't see into the room, could you?"

"No. I wanted to get out of the line of fire. I backed against the wall and called them out."

"Did Crowder come out right away?"

"No. When he did come out he said he'd looked at Ed and I'd killed him."

"So he'd have had time to pick up the guns and throw them out of the window?"

"Plenty." He scowled and wiped the sweat from his face.

"You know what I think happened, Amy. I think it now. I didn't then. I think I surprised them. They wanted to have me covered when I came in. That's why Ed went for his gun—too late to cover me."

"How could you know that then?"

"I couldn't. If they'd pulled the curtains and had a gun on me when I opened the door it never would have happened."

Amy nodded and then said quietly, "You don't belong here, Cam. Ben had no business locking you up."

She stood up now and so did Cam. "I'm going to try him again," Amy said determinedly.

"Tell me something," Cam said quietly. "You don't like bounty hunters and you don't like killing, I'm guilty on both counts. Why do you care what happens to me?"

Amy regarded him with a puzzled frown before she answered. "Why, it's the principle of the thing, I guess. I don't think Ben has clear evidence of your guilt. I think you shot at a man you thought was going to shoot you. I'd do the same thing if Crowder was in your place." She hesitated. "No, I don't guess I would. Not after that beating he gave you."

Now she blushed and said firmly, "Besides, do you have to have a reason?"

"No, but thanks."

Amy smiled, walked across the cell, rattled the cell door, and called, "Ben, Ben, let me out."

While she waited for Judd she turned and said to Cam, "Is there anything I can get you?"

"Just ask Ben if he'll bring me my blanket roll."

Judd came in the cellblock then and unlocked the cell door and let Amy out, relocking it after she was in the walkway. Cam had another drink from the canteen and then lay down on the cot with his hands locked behind his head.

He was still not quite over his surprise at Amy's visit. She was a strange, stubborn, but, above all, fair girl. He was certain she disliked what he was doing and especially what he was doing to Tina but she had fought for his rights against the man she would probably marry. It didn't add up, but still in his heart he was grateful to her.

He did not know how long he had slept when he heard footsteps in the walkway and came awake. It was Ben Judd with his blanket roll and now Judd opened the door, pitched in the blanket roll, and relocked the cell door.

Grasping one of the cell bars in each hand he looked sternly at Cam, who now sat up.

"That's quite a job you did on Amy."

"Did I lie to her?"

The sheriff ignored the question; he said, "She thinks I ought to let you out."

"So do I."

"Well, I won't. You killed an unarmed man needlessly, in my opinion. If the district attorney doesn't think so he'll order you freed. But he'll have to do it. I won't."

When the sheriff had left Cam went over to the canteen, doused his head with water, took a drink, and sat down on the cot. It was obvious that Amy's siding with him had only increased the sheriff's stubbornness. If he'd ever had any doubts as to the rightness of Cam's arrest, they disappeared in the face of Amy's actions. In a way Cam felt sorry for Sheriff Ben Judd. Besides a town full of bounty hunters to contend with he now had a murder on his hands. Normally, Cam supposed, a ten-minute talk with the district attorney would inform the sheriff exactly what he should do, but in the district attorney's absence Judd was playing it safe.

And what about the district attorney, Cam wondered? Was he some unread jackleg lawyer who wanted to play it safe too? What guarantee was there that after the district attorney returned he would free him. What if the man decided to bind him over for trial?

Cam lay back on the cot and stared at the ceiling. His plan to decoy Chance into moving toward the gold had backfired, for sure. His only hope was if Chance, cocky and self-confident, would take his time about moving out—four days to be exact.

9

It wasn't until midafternoon that Rufe, the ramrod of Wes Chance's Mexican crew, got around to picking up the mail. Back at Chance's place he left the sparse mail on Chance's desk and went about his business. An hour later Chance came in, tossed what he knew were feed bills aside, then opened Tina's envelope.

Standing before his desk he opened the envelope of Tom Yates's letter, read the letter and Tina's note. Then he sat down in his swivel chair and reread both the letter and the note. Only on the second reading did the full impact of the Yates letter reach him. So one of the passengers on the train that night thought he recognized him and wanted Tina to confirm it.

Chance cursed softly and he felt fear touch him and then slowly subside. He didn't know who this Yates was and didn't propose to try and hunt him down with the town full of bounty hunters. He himself had been into town, the business district of it, only three or four times since the bullion robbery. The last time had been a couple of days ago. It was possible that Yates had spotted him and followed him back to the horse corral.

Tina, that beautiful, greedy little slut, had handled this properly, but Chance could see what lay ahead for him. If Tina answered Yates's letter and agreed to accompany him on the identification and told Yates he had the wrong man there was still trouble ahead.

Without question Yates would go to Carpenter with his hunch and bargain for a reward, however modest. Carpenter, in turn, would pick up the sheriff and come here to question him. Tina would be brought into it and even though she denied this was the man she had seen on the train, the suspicion would still linger in the sheriff's mind. It would be the only real lead that the sheriff had and Carpenter would dog him into investigating every move Chance had made. To sum it up he would be under suspicion and probably surveillance, as would Tina.

Chance came to his decision then. Neither he nor Tina could be investigated if they weren't here to be questioned by Carpenter and the sheriff. The thing to do was pick up Tina, head for the gold, and then move into Mexico.

His mind made up, Chance left the office for the corral, caught Cam's dun, saddled him, and set out for the Bowers house. If anybody was curious as to the reason for his visit his answer would be that Dan Bowers owed him money and he was trying to collect it from Mrs. Bowers.

At the Bowers house he knocked on the front door and the back door and could not rouse Tina. Had she gone back to the Kimballs at Diamond K, he wondered? Before he made the ride out there, however, there was an easier way to check.

He rode into the business district, reined in at Johnson's, and tramped through the store back to the post office. Of the gray-haired woman behind the wicket, Johnson's wife whom he did not know, he asked, "Who's picking up the mail for Mrs. Dan Bowers nowadays?"

"Why, Amy Cross takes it. She's Mrs. Bowers' neighbor, you know."

As Chance rode back to his place he reflected on Mrs. Johnson's information. If Amy Cross was picking up Tina's mail then Tina couldn't be at the Diamond K, for it would be simple enough for Lew Kimball to pick up her mail at the post office instead of going through Amy Cross. It must mean that Tina was in town.

Chance spent the rest of the afternoon preparing to travel. In an empty, heavy canvas *aparejo* he put the blankets, filled canteen, food, and cooking utensils that he and Tina would need once they had picked up the bullion. The gold would go in the *aparejo* and the rest of the gear and blankets behind their saddles. He cut out a sturdy pack mule, fed him, and tied him to the water trough so he would be readily available.

He took his supper as usual in the two-room adobe of one of his Mexican horse wranglers whose wife earned a fair wage for feeding him. Afterward he went to his office to wait until dark.

Sitting at his desk he wondered what would happen to his small business when he was gone. Probably Rufe would take over, get the horses and mules from Mexico, pay the crew, and wonder what had happened to his boss. As for the investment here, he could afford to write it off. At most he had a few hundred dollars in buildings and horseflesh. Compared to what he would take into Mexico in bullion it was a pittance.

At full dark he saddled up the dun and again rode over to the Bowers house. He noted lights in the Cross house as he rode by. Again he knocked on the front and rear doors of the Bowers house, but not long enough to attract the attention of the Crosses. He got no answer again. If Tina was inside the dark house she wasn't answering any knocks on the door.

Methodically then, Chance went to the side of the house the farthest from the Crosses', quietly broke a window with the butt of his gun, unlocked the window, raised the sash, and moved into the house. His search there was very thorough, and before he was finished he knew that Tina was not staying here. His search finished, he went out through the window and contemplated his next move.

If Amy Cross was picking up Tina's mail, then it was reasonable to go to the Crosses', say that Mrs. Johnson told him that Amy was picking up Tina's mail and that he was looking for her because Dan Bowers owed him a debt he wanted to collect. Could Amy Cross tell him where he could find Mrs. Bowers? he would ask.

As he moved toward the Crosses' he saw the turned-down lamp in the front window but there was bright lamplight in what he gathered was the kitchen, so he headed for the back door. Approaching the rear of the house he looked through the window and saw William Cross seated at the kitchen table writing. Chance halted and presently Amy came over to her father, put a hand on his shoulder, and spoke to him.

While she was still speaking Tina Bowers came in from the adjoining room. She was in a gray wrapper and her hair was pinned atop her head as if she had just finished bathing.

For a moment Chance was puzzled and then the scene made some sense to him. The Crosses had taken in Tina, probably to spare her the pestering of the bounty hunters; in other words she was living at the Crosses'. It would be impossible, rash, and foolish of him to try and see her tonight. Tomorrow morning, of course, both Amy and William Cross would be at the *Times* office and Tina would be alone. He could wait.

Next morning Chance took his time about saddling the dun and a second horse, and loading the packsaddle on the mule. He wanted to give Amy Cross and her father plenty of time to reach the *Times* office.

Afterward, when he judged it to be past eight o'clock, he rode out of the horse lot, leading the mule and Tina's horse under the incurious stares of Rufe and the crew. He seldom told them where he was going or when he would return and they accepted his departure as only routine.

Shortly he was in the alley behind the Cross house and here he dismounted and tied the mule and the two mounts to the back fence. Afterward, he went up the walk, climbed the steps, and walked boldly through the back door without knocking.

Hearing his footsteps Tina called from another room, "Is that you, Lew?"

"Come out here," Chance commanded.

In a moment Tina appeared and said sharply, "What are you doing here, Wes? How did you know I was here?"

"Saw you through the window last night. Got any riding clothes here?"

Tina unconsciously looked down at her dark housedress and then said, "Why yes. But why?"

"Go get 'em," Chance said. "I'll follow you."

"What on earth are you talking about?" Tina demanded.

"You're coming with me. You're not going to write to Tom

Yates or see him or talk with him. Now go get your clothes, bring them down here, and change in the kitchen."

"While you watch? I won't do it."

Chance moved up to her and gave her a backhanded blow across her face. Tina staggered back, surprise and fear in her face, and raised a hand to her cheek. Chance raised a hand, fingers outspread, then slowly fisted them. "Next time it'll be this."

"Where are you taking me?" Tina asked, a quaver in her voice.

"Mainly, away from here. For the last time now, get your clothes."

Tina turned and left the room, Chance on her heels. Upstairs, still under his watchful gaze, she took down her riding clothes and boots and hat from the closet and then led the way down to the kitchen.

Once there Chance said, "All right. Undress and change. I won't watch you, if that's worrying you."

While she changed out of her housedress into a divided skirt, blouse, and cowman's boots Chance looked out the window. When she was finished she said, "All right, now what?"

"You've got pencil and paper here. Go and get them and bring them here."

Chance again followed her into the living room where she got pencil and paper and they both returned to the kitchen. "Write a note to the Crosses," Chance said. "Tell them you're going out to the Diamond K for a few days."

Obediently, Tina sat down at the kitchen table and wrote the note Chance had ordered. In her mind, however, was pure panic. Cam was in jail and would be for four or five days or even longer, Amy had said last night. The fake letter from Tom Yates had succeeded in moving Chance out of town, but who was there to follow him now and track him down and find the gold?

When she finished, Chance said, "Leave it right there. They'll see it. Now come on."

"Can I take some things with me?" Tina asked.

"Yes, the dress you took off, and a comb. I've got blankets and grub. That's all you'll need."

Again, with Chance following, she went upstairs and got a comb and a couple of handkerchiefs, then led the way back into the kitchen. There Chance took over and led her outside to the three mounts in the alley.

When Tina's stirrups were adjusted, Chance mounted and they started down the alley toward the east edge of town. Once there, they circled south into the roadless waste of desert.

10

An hour after Chance and Tina had left the Crosses', Lew Kimball rode up to the Cross place, walked to the front door, and knocked. Receiving no answer he thought Tina must be in the rear, so he circled the house and again knocked and got no answer.

He turned now and looked across the way at Tina's house. Now that things had subsided a little maybe she had moved back into her house. Accordingly, he walked over to Tina's house and knocked on the back door. There was no answer. He tried the door and found it was locked. Now he circled the house, heading for the front door. He was walking past the bedroom window when his boots crunched glass and he halted, looking down first at the ground and then up at the window. He could see where the window had been smashed, unlocked, and raised.

Kimball stood there frowning. Had some prowler, noticing the house continued to be dark, broken in and looted it?

Kimball was a thorough man. Now he proved it. He went around to the front door, tried the lock, saw the door was barred, came back to the broken window, pulled his gun, and climbed through the window into the bedroom.

In his careful search of the house he could see that nothing, apparently, was missing, although he couldn't be sure. Certainly, Tina wasn't living here now. The beds were made, the kitchen was cleaned up, and there was a film of dust on the tables and chairs.

Besides being a thorough man, Kimball was a clever man. There had to be an answer to where Tina was. Now, because this house showed no signs of life, he left it by the bedroom window and retraced his steps to the rear door of the Crosses'. When his knock again went unanswered he tried the doorknob and found the door unlocked.

Swinging it open, he moved into the kitchen and called, "Tina! Tina, where are you?"

The house was silent and now Kimball's glance fell to the sheet of paper on the kitchen table. Moving over to it he saw that it was addressed to Amy and signed by Tina. Without hesitation, he read the note Tina had left. Finished, he knew immediately that it was impossible Tina had gone out to the Diamond K. He had been there until an hour ago and there was only one road from El Cuervo to the ranch and he would have passed Tina. It was her handwriting on the message, all right, but the contents didn't make sense.

Now Kimball made a quick search of the house and, of course, found nothing. Once in the kitchen he folded Tina's note, pocketed it, went out of the back door, circled the house, mounted his horse, and headed for the business district.

As he rode past the Cameo the usual crowd of bounty hunters, ducking the midday heat, were whooping it up. But Kimball thought there was a little less noise than there had been a couple of days ago. He rode on to the *Times* office, dismounted, went inside, and waited an impatient two minutes while Amy, behind the counter, got rid of a salesman. William Cross, back at the handpress, did not see him.

When Amy came up to him she smiled and said, "I'm sorry, Lew, but we have to see these people."

Lew nodded. He reached in his shirt pocket, took out Tina's note, and then covered it with his hand, saying, "No apologies, Amy. I went into your house to try and find Tina. I found this note on your kitchen table and read it." He took his hands off the note and let Amy read what was written there.

Amy finished, looked up and smiled and said, "Oh, I am so glad, Lew. I'm afraid our house was getting pretty confining."

"Then she hasn't been out? She hasn't been around town?"

"She hasn't been out of the house for two days."

Lew said grimly, "Better call your father, Amy. Something's up."

Amy gave him a puzzled look, then went back and when she was past the desk called, "Dad, Lew's here to see us."

William Cross, collar open, shirt sleeves up, picked up a rag and started for the counter, wiping his hands as he came. He nodded to Lew Kimball, who said, "Better read this, William, and see what you make of it."

He told about calling at the Crosses', not finding Tina, going over to Tina's house, searching it, and finding nothing for his pains except a broken window where somebody had entered. Now William Cross read the letter and said, "Where did this come from?"

"I found it on your kitchen table. I went back to your house again looking for Tina and there it was. Tina's gone."

"To your place, it says," William Cross said.

"She's not there and on my way into town I didn't meet her. If she was coming to our place I'd have seen her."

"Any signs of violence in either our place or hers?" Amy asked.

"None at all. The beds were made up in both places and the kitchens were clean."

"Where would she get a horse?" Amy asked, and there was a beginning fright in her amber eyes.

"Holgate's? She rode his horse in, maybe he came by and wanted to talk with her and then gave her his horse."

"Cam Holgate is in jail—held for murder," Amy said grimly.

Kimball listened with lips parted in disbelief as Amy described briefly and angrily what had happened at Cam's hotel yesterday. She told of Ben Judd's careless and seemingly biased handling of the whole incident. She finished by saying, "Ben is determined to wait till Riley gets back from San Isbel. He won't move without the district attorney's consent and approval."

"Why didn't I know about this?" Kimball finally said. "Why didn't you send word out to me?"

"What was the use, Lew? You couldn't have done anything, any more than we could."

William Cross said, "I suggest we lock up the shop, Amy, and go talk with Ben, along with Lew. Maybe he'll have some ideas."

"Maybe Cam will too. Remember he and Tina were partners."

Lew and Amy waited in the heat outside the *Times* office while William Cross locked up and joined them. The three of them walked down to the blessed shade of the *portal* in front of the sheriff's office and turned into it.

Ben Judd was alone at his desk doing paper work when he heard them enter. He turned and then, surprise on his face, rose and said, "What is it now, Amy? Are you rallying your forces, like they say in the army."

"It's something besides Cam, Ben. Tell him, Lew."

While Kimball, standing, told the sheriff about his search for Tina and showed him the note that Tina had left, Amy sat down in the straight chair by the desk and William Cross leaned a shoulder against the wall. When Kimball finished the sheriff, standing too, said, "Are you saying it was kidnapping, Lew?"

"I'm not saying anything except she wasn't at her place or the Crosses' and she isn't at my place. Where is she?"

"What do you want of her?" the sheriff asked.

Amy said, half angrily, "Oh, quit it, Ben! Lew and Tina are relatives. Why shouldn't he drop in to talk to her and see how she's doing?"

"I just wondered if he had any special message for her that we could use, is all," Ben said to Amy in an aggrieved tone.

"None," Kimball said. "I just wanted to say hello."

Now the sheriff half sat on his desk and reread Tina's note, tugging at his long mustaches in a way that irritated Amy again. He looked up at Kimball, "You're sure this is her handwriting?"

"I'm sure," Amy said. "And Lew accepted it. Why don't you?"

"I'm only asking," the sheriff said patiently.

"Why don't you ask Cam Holgate about Tina? They were partners. He might know something you don't," Amy said.

"Like what?" the sheriff asked dryly.

"I don't know," Amy's voice held impatience. "Just tell him. Or have Lew tell him what happened today."

The sheriff pushed himself erect and said, "All right, come on, Lew. Let's talk with him."

"For heaven's sake, Ben, bring Cam out here. It's three times as hot in there as it is here and it's hell in here," Amy said sharply.

"All right," Ben said meekly. He took down the key ring, moved over to the cellblock door, opened it, and went inside. He was gone just long enough to let Cam put on his boots and a shirt.

Cam was first to come through the cellblock door. His shirt was already wringing wet and his face looked haggard. However, the heat in the cellblock must have acted as an enforced poultice for his hurt face, for the bruises were fading and the swelling around his mouth had almost disappeared.

Cam halted just inside the office and looked at the three of them and then smiled at Amy.

Now the sheriff took over. He said, "Take my chair, Holgate, and listen to what Lew Kimball has to tell you."

Cam moved over to the chair and slacked into it, looked briefly at Amy and then at Lew. "How are the twins?" he asked.

Kimball smiled and said, "Same as ever. Full of mischief."

The sheriff interrupted. "Go on, Lew."

For the third time Lew Kimball described the circumstances of Tina's disappearance. As Kimball talked the sheriff watched Cam and Cam tried to keep his face impassive. He felt anything but impassive, however. Wes Chance was on the move and probably, for safety's sake, had taken Tina with him. The forged letter from Tom Yates had worked only too well, Cam thought bitterly.

When Kimball had finished the sheriff said, "What do you make of it, Holgate?"

Cam said slowly, looking at the sheriff, "I think your bullion robber took her away so she couldn't identify him."

"How do you know that?" the sheriff asked swiftly.

"I don't. I'm guessing. Who else would want her and for what other reason?"

"How would he know where to look for her, Cam?" Amy asked.

"Well, the broken window of her house says he was looking for her." Cam frowned then and looking at Amy asked, "Do you pull down your shades at night?"

"Only in the bedrooms," Amy said.

"Then couldn't he have looked through a window and seen Tina in your place?"

"Why, after dark, very easily," Amy answered.

"He'd have to know something about you and your father too, wouldn't he?"

"What's that supposed to mean?" Judd asked sourly.

"That he'd have to know Amy and her father work at the *Times* office all day and wouldn't be home this morning. He'd have to bring a horse for Tina or a rig. He couldn't be seen walking through town with her, could he? Have you had a look at the place, sheriff?"

"I knew about this three minutes before you did," the sheriff answered sourly.

"All right. But when neither of us have seen Amy's house since Tina was taken out of it why are you asking me for the answers?" Cam said.

"That's true, Ben," Amy said swiftly. "Cam has made some reasonable guesses so why don't you take him to our house and let him look around?"

The sheriff flushed. "Anything he can see, I can see."

"Well, you couldn't see who could have taken Tina and Cam could. Besides, you'll have a gun and he won't. Are you afraid?"

William Cross said, "Easy does it, Amy."

The sheriff looked at Amy with anger and then said, "All right, Holgate, we'll go."

"Walking?"

"It's not far," the sheriff said.

"It's too far for me. The way I feel, I'd never make it there and back."

"I suppose you'd like me to carry you on my back," Judd said sardonically.

"No. I hadn't thought of that," Cam said. "But I've got a horse down at the feed stable that'll carry me."

"All right. Get back in your cell, I'll get your horse."

The sheriff locked Cam in his cell again and Cam moved over and sat down on the cot, his heart still pounding with excitement. Thanks to Amy Cross's contrariness he had found a way out of here. He silently blessed her. In a few minutes he would have a horse, his hat—protection against the murderous sun—was on the cot, and with luck he could get the sheriff's gun. The only unknown factor was Kimball. Would he side with the sheriff or would he side with him? Cam had a feeling that Kimball wouldn't fight him. That left only the question of water and Cam gave this some close thought.

The canteen the sheriff had given him this morning had been emptied long since and Cam was thirsty now. Only a sort of cussedness had kept him from calling the sheriff to fill his canteen; he had wondered how long it would take Ben Judd to wonder how his water supply was. Right now that was an advantage. His scheme might work, but on the other hand Judd might get both stubborn and suspicious.

Ten minutes later the sheriff came into the cellblock. Cam put on his hat, picked up the canteen, and waited while the sheriff unlocked the door. The sheriff stood aside and Cam stepped out into the walkway. The sheriff backed off a step, put his hand on his gun, and said, "What's the canteen for?"

"It's been empty for five hours. I'm thirsty."

The sheriff held out his hand. "I forgot. I'm sorry. Give it to me."

Cam handed the canteen to him and said, "Do me a small

favor, will you, sheriff? Your water here starts out warm and winds up hot. Will you fill that canteen at the Cross house?"

Surprisingly, the sheriff said, "All right," and gestured toward the door.

Cam walked slowly through the office as if he were very tired, went out to the boardwalk under the *portal,* saw his horse tied at the tie rail, and moved toward it. The sheriff mounted his own horse at the same time Cam mounted his and Cam noticed with satisfaction that the sheriff had the canteen slung by its strap over the horn of the saddle.

They rode down the dusty street, threading their way past wagon traffic and the big ore wagons. When they came to the alley behind the Cross house the sheriff started to turn into it and Cam said, "Wait a minute, sheriff."

Judd reined in and looked curiously at him.

"Let's go round to the front. There may be tracks there in the alley that'll tell us something."

The sheriff nodded and they went down to the cross street and up to the front door of the Cross house. Dismounting and tying their horses to the small tie rail the sheriff motioned Cam to go round the house ahead of him. Cam said, "Don't forget the canteen, sheriff," and then tramped around the corner of the porch with the sheriff, canteen in hand, following him.

The back door was open and Amy and Lew Kimball were sitting at the kitchen table.

Without speaking Cam went directly to the hand pump at the sink, picked up a tin cup beside it and pumped a cupful of water, drank it down, and pumped another cup and drank that down. Afterward he turned, extended his hand and said, "I'll fill it," to the sheriff.

The sheriff gave him the canteen and Cam pumped it full, capped it, then laid it on the sink counter.

"All right, Master Detective, what's our first move?" the sheriff asked sarcastically.

Cam looked at Amy and said, "Amy, when Tina came home and then here the first night she was wearing riding clothes. Can you check and see if they're gone?"

Amy nodded, rose and left the room.

Cam walked past the sheriff now toward the back door saying, "Let's have a look out here."

Cam led the way down the back walk, the sheriff behind him and Kimball trailing. Where the walk ended at the gateless gap in the back fence Cam halted, then very carefully studied the tracks in the dust of the alley. He could see the two sets of boot tracks, one large, one small and he pointed to them, saying, "Tina's tracks and a man's tracks."

Then he lifted his arm and pointed to the fresh horse dung in the alley and said, "That's where he tied their horses. Better stay here until I call you over."

Cam was almost certain what the tracks by the fence would tell him, but in spite of it his heart was beating faster. He walked carefully over to where the horses had been tethered and then knelt down to examine the tracks. The first set of tracks nearest the walk told him what he wanted to know. There in the dust were the distinctive tracks of the dun he had sold Wes Chance.

He circled these tracks and gave a careful look at the other two sets of tracks, concentrating on the tracks of the middle horse, not the dun. Then he waved the sheriff and Kimball over. They walked over the dun's tracks, Cam noticed. When they were beside him, Cam knelt down and said, "You'll have to look close, sheriff."

The sheriff stepped over to Cam's right side in order to have his gun on the far side of Cam and then he knelt. Kimball, almost incurious, stood on the other side of Cam, listening.

Now Cam pointed to the tracks of the middle horse in the dust and said, "Notice those hind shoes, sheriff? They're narrower than the shoes on the other two horses. Lean over and take a good look."

As the sheriff leaned over, Cam laced the fingers of both hands into one huge fist and then, as the sheriff bent down and reached out to touch the track he was examining, Cam raised his hands swiftly and even more swiftly brought them down on the back of the sheriff's neck.

The sheriff grunted and pitched forward in the dust, unconscious.

Now Cam looked up at Kimball, whose hand was on the butt of his gun. "Don't do it, Lew," Cam said. "I'm going to take his gun and you give me yours, so it will look as if I disarmed you with his gun. He can't come back at you."

Without waiting for an answer, Cam rolled the sheriff on his back, unbuckled his shell belt, pulled it out from under him, and then strapped the shell belt and holstered gun around his own waist.

"What're you going to do, Cam?"

"I'm going to track these horses, Lew, because I think the killer's riding one. I'm going to find him, Tina, and the gold." He held out his hand, "Do you want to give me your gun? It'll save the sheriff combing you over, and you know it."

Kimball was smiling as he lifted the gun from its holster and extended it to Cam. "He'll be one mad sheriff, I reckon. Now what?"

"The canteen in the kitchen, and I'm off."

Kimball looked at him, nodded and then said, "You know I think you know what you're doing. Good luck, fella."

Cam hurried up the walk, moved into the kitchen, picked up the canteen, and had turned to go out when Amy's voice came from the doorway into the next room. "Cam! Where are you going?"

Cam halted. "Ask Lew, but not in front of Ben. I'm sorry I had to hit Ben, Amy. Now don't go out to see Lew for a whole minute."

He went out of the door, rounded the house, jogged toward his horse, reached him, slipped the canteen strap over the saddle horn, mounted, pulled his horse around, put him into a gallop past Tina's house, then at the end of that empty block he turned left and picked up the alley again. Here he turned right and headed east out of town. The freshest tracks in the alley were those of his dun along with two other horses. The depression of a dry arroyo put him out of sight of Kimball, and the tracks of Chance's horse and Tina's and the third horse turned south in this arroyo.

11

Amy waited the minute that Cam had specified, then stepped out of the door, halted, saw Lew Kimball kneeling beside Ben, and then ran down the walk and out into the alley.

Halting beside Lew, she said, "What happened? Is he hurt?"

Kimball rose and then said, "Cam slugged him. He put Ben's gun on me, took my gun, picked up his canteen, ran around the house, and that's the last I saw of him."

"Where was he going, Lew?"

"After Tina, he said. Her, the killer, and the gold."

Amy brushed by him and knelt by Ben, who was still unconscious. She looked up at Kimball and said, "Get some water, Lew. Maybe it'll bring him around."

"On my way," Kimball said. He went up the walk and into the kitchen and presently returned with a pitcher of water drawn from the pump.

Amy took the water, then reached in her pocket for her handkerchief, folded it over Ben's nose and then gently poured the cold water over his face and neck and eyes and forehead. Judd moved, opened his eyes, pawed the handkerchief away from his nostrils, and then came up on an elbow.

"What happened?" the sheriff asked. "I know Holgate hit me. But where is he?"

Lew explained then that Holgate had slugged him, grabbed his gun, covered Lew, took his gun, went into the house, got the canteen, and was off.

By the time he was finished Judd was sitting up and now he

came unsteadily to his feet. "Did you see him, Amy?" Judd said.

"I was looking over Tina's clothes. When I came out you were lying in the alley here and Lew was kneeling beside you."

"Which way did he go, Lew?"

"I honestly can't tell you, Ben," Kimball answered. "He put his horse into a gallop and it sounded as if he went east."

"Why didn't you ride after him?"

"I walked Amy here, Ben."

"My horse was out in front. Why didn't you take him?"

"How do I capture him? With my bare hands? Besides he was your prisoner, not mine. You're the one that let him out of jail, I didn't."

The two men looked at each other. There was almost hatred in Judd's eyes as he wiped his wet face with the sleeve of his shirt. Kimball's eyes held a kind of friendly malice as he regarded the sheriff.

Now Amy said, "You two stop quarreling. Nobody could help what happened."

Sullenly, the sheriff bent down, picked up his hat, put it on, and then said to Amy, "It was your idea to bring him here. How do you like it?"

"I like it fine," Amy said flatly. "He didn't belong in jail in the first place."

"So you hoped he'd escape, is that it?"

"You're being damned unfair, Ben," Amy said hotly. "How did I know he'd try to escape? You didn't."

The sheriff shifted his glance. "What did you make about what he said about those tracks, Lew?"

"I think he wanted to get you down on your knees so he could slug you."

"So do I," the sheriff said sourly.

The sheriff looked at where the tracks had been. In his fall and in the dousing of water by Amy on his face, the tracks that he had been looking at were obliterated. Slowly now, he walked out into the alley trying to pick up the narrow shoe track Cam had pointed out. He thought he found one print in the alley dust and walked another twenty yards east before he picked up a doubtful one. Returning to Amy and Lew, he said in a discouraged voice, "It'd take me to dark to track them to the edge of town. It's hopeless."

"No posse?" Kimball asked.

The sheriff shook his head in negation. "By the time I get the men rounded up and provisioned, it'll be the middle of the afternoon. If we get someone that can track them, he'll have to quit at dark. They'll travel all night and be out of reach by morning."

"But Cam can't track in the dark, either," Amy said.

"What makes you think he's tracking?"

"Why, he's bounty hunting, isn't he?" Amy said.

"He's running away from a murder charge," the sheriff said flatly. "He knows if he got the bullion and the killer and turned them in to Carpenter I'd have him. No, he's gone."

Amy gave him a searching look and then shrugged and said, "Let's get out of this sun." She turned and headed for the house.

"Anything I can do, Ben?" Kimball asked.

"Not right now, Lew."

Kimball called, " 'By, Amy," and then said to Judd, "See you later, Ben," and started down the alley toward the business district.

Judd watched Amy a moment and then followed her into the kitchen. Amy was at the sink pump washing off the alley dust from the pitcher. As she was wiping water off the pitcher, her back to him, Judd said heavily, "We've got to have a talk, Amy."

Amy turned and looked at him. "All right," she said calmly. "Why don't we sit down?"

Judd took off his hat, walked over to the kitchen table, and took a chair. Amy crossed over to the table and took the chair opposite him. "Talk about what?" Amy said.

Judd tugged at his mustaches and eyed Amy somberly. "Ever since this Holgate hit town he's mixing up in our lives, Amy. Who asked him to?"

Amy thought a moment and then said, "Why, it just happened, Ben. I suppose Tina was really the cause of it. We wanted to help her, so did he, and then all these things happened."

"But you always seem to be taking his side against me."

"That's not true, Ben," Amy said with spirit. "I just don't think you've been fair with him."

"I think I have. Still, what gravels me is that it's always my judgment against yours and his."

"It was your judgment that he should come here and look around."

Judd leaned forward. "Amy, Amy, open your eyes. The minute Lew told Holgate about Tina's disappearance he started an escape plot. Think back on it. He's the one who said he thought the killer kidnapped Tina. He's the one who asked if I'd looked around the place. You helped him there by asking why I didn't take him here. Then he got too exhausted to walk so I got him a horse. Even that empty canteen was a piece of trickery. He wanted to get out of jail, he needed a horse, he needed water, he needed a gun, and he got mine." He leaned back in his chair. "I think I've been fair with him. Way too fair."

In spite of her conviction that she had acted rightly, Amy felt a sense of guilt. Ben had shown up poorly in all his dealings with Holgate and he was conscious that he had. When word got around that Holgate had escaped from him the town would jeer at him behind his back. No law officer, especially a young one, wants to be known as ineffective, Amy knew. The *Times* would have to publish the account of Holgate's escape and that would be even more humiliating to Ben, since the whole town knew he was going to marry Amy Cross.

It was as if Ben was reading her thoughts as he asked quietly, "Does this have to get into the *Times,* Amy?"

"It happened, didn't it? If it happened to another sheriff we'd print it."

Ben's eyes held so much of quiet pleading that Amy's glance fell. Ben said, "But with the edgy feeling in the town now with all these drunken bounty hunters. They might think they can get away with anything, with me and the night marshal. It could just stir up trouble, Amy, and plenty of it."

"You mean it's not to the public interest to print it. Is that what you're saying, Ben?"

"Something like that."

"I'll talk with dad about it. He's the boss."

Ben's forearms were on the table, his hands loosely clasped and now impulsively Amy reached out and put her hand on his. "Oh Ben, don't take it so personally. Every day somebody in this country breaks out of jail. It just happens."

"Not out of my jail," Judd said gloomily.

Amy withdrew her hand and her forehead puckered in a frown as she looked at a point over Judd's shoulders, thinking some unpleasant thoughts and then deciding to voice them. She said, "Would it help, Ben, if we printed that you had had some second thoughts about Cam's being arrested for that killing? That you'd decided you couldn't legally hold him? That would explain why you took him out of jail, got his horse, and gave him water. The reason you came here with him was because you thought he could help solve Tina's disappearance."

Judd was silent, thinking this over. "Why did he slug me, Amy?"

"Nobody knows what you two talked about when you were riding over here. Maybe you told him you were running him out of town and out of the country. He got mad. He needed a gun so he hit you and took yours."

Judd looked at her searchingly. He opened his mouth to speak, closed it, frowned, and then finally spoke. "So I freed the prisoner; he didn't escape. He hit me because he was sore over being kept in jail all this time. Is that it?"

"If you said all this, we'd have to print it," Amy said. "The only one that could deny it would be Cam and you say he's on the run and won't come back."

"There's Lew and your father, Amy. They heard."

"Not what you and Cam talked about on the way over here. Only you two know that."

"Think Lew will tell what he knows?"

"Lew doesn't know and I don't know and Dad doesn't know what you and Holgate talked about in the jail when you freed him and when you rode over here."

Judd tugged at his mustache again and then suddenly smiled, got up, came over to Amy, tilted up her chin, and kissed her. "All right, girl. That's the story I gave the *Times*. Now I've got to go." He kissed her again and then moved through the house toward his horse out front.

Amy heard the door close and sat there, staring at nothing. She had trapped Ben and she despised herself for it. But that didn't alter the facts. Presented with the idea of and a chance to lie himself out of a humiliating situation, he had decided to accept. If only, instead of smiling and kissing her and agreeing to the deception, he had brought down his fists on the table and said, "No, Amy, these are lies. I'll take my medicine. Write the truth." But he hadn't.

Step by step he had silently approved each of the deceptions, first making sure they were plausible. In the end he had agreed to this enormous lie. Was this the real Ben Judd she had promised to marry—an overproud man too cowardly to face the truth that had happened to him?

Despite the heat of the room, she shivered. Well, she would write the story in the *Times* as she had promised him. If her father saw the flaws in it she would send him to Ben. She hoped bitterly that Cam would return and denounce Ben. But even if he didn't Amy knew that shortly she would return Ben's ring to him. They would both know why, without her having to explain it.

Now, remembering Ben's departure, she raised an arm and scrubbed her lips with the sleeve of her dress as if to wipe away his kisses.

12

Cam guessed that at most, Chance and Tina had a four-hour head start on him. It took Cam less than half an hour to determine the direction Chance was heading. Chance paid no attention to the lie of the land or the natural and easy grade for the horses. He was headed, so far as Cam could make out, in the direction of a low range of mountains directly east.

The natural thing for Chance to assume was that he was not being followed so he wouldn't keep an extra careful eye on his back trail. Still, Cam didn't want to take any chances. He moved his horse a half mile to the north and rode steadily through the increasing heat of the day.

This was an arid rolling country of mesquite, cactus, and what few trails and even fewer roads that crossed it Chance carefully avoided. This made tracking him much easier and every hour Cam would drift back, pick up the tracks, and then move off either south or north.

During these long hours in the saddle Cam had a chance to assess his situation. He was fairly certain that the sheriff hadn't picked up the unique tracks made by his dun that Chance was probably riding. Even if he had, tracking would be painfully slow and would stop when dark came. The sheriff, of course, had a choice to make. Would he think kidnapping a more serious affair than an escaped prisoner at large? Would he consider riding herd on a bunch of drunken bounty hunters more important than hunting down Tina or hunting down his escaped prisoner?

In midafternoon Cam spotted the light green of some paloverde trees and angled toward them, knowing there was water there and where there was water there were people.

He came on a cluster of adobes around a walled-in seep, with a brush sheep corral off to the side. There seemed to be only women and children here and in bad Spanish he bargained with the Mexican women for food. He left with his saddlebags stuffed with jerky and tamales, and oats for his horse, and again headed north to pick up the tracks.

Approaching the low line of hills in midafternoon he knew he would have to halt until dark. From the height of the hills Chance would most certainly watch his back trail and the whole sweep of the country would lie below him. The sight of even a lone rider would alert him.

Cam found a deep arroyo that would hide him and his horse in a sliver of shade that would increase as the sun heeled over. He fed and watered his horse; then, his back against the arroyo wall, he ate his jerky and tamales.

He thought of what lay ahead. He had Chance's line of travel which was aimed directly at the highest peak of the mountains. It would show on the night horizon and this would be his objective, come dark. Once on the peak he had the best opportunity to pick out the horizon stars. Saddling up, he started out on what he knew would be a slow journey. In daylight he could see the lie of the land and avoid the steep-walled arroyos or find a way to cross them. In darkness he had to trust to his horse, and this meant slow going.

In a couple of hours he had achieved the base of the peak he was aiming at. As he climbed he left the true desert behind him and was in a country of stunted cedar and *piñon* whose presence he confirmed by raking his hand through a branch and smelling needles in his palm. This was rougher country and he had to absolutely trust his horse to find a way through it.

It was long after midnight and halfway up the slope to the peak when he caught a smell that made him rein his horse in. Over the crude smell of his long unwashed prison stench and the odor of his perspiring horse he smelled the faint but unmistakable odor of wood smoke. It had the light, distinct smell of smoldering *piñon* wood.

As noiselessly as he could he turned his horse and put it down the back trail until even the faintest smell of the smoke was gone. Reining in then, he dismounted and pondered the situation. There was no guarantee that he was smelling the smoke from Chance's fire. There was no reason Chance wouldn't have built a fire earlier against the chill of the night and Chance had no reason to believe that a fire would give him away to anyone. Chance would have reasoned, and rightly, that Tina's absence wouldn't be noticed until the Crosses came home for their noon meal. If they believed her note, and there was no reason they shouldn't, then there was very likely nobody at all on his back trail, so why not build a fire? Why not build a big one and bank it with logs against the chill of the night?

What sort of a camp would Chance make with Tina? First he would picket the horses well away from the camp, probably hobble them. In the darkness he would likely hide the saddles and bridles in another place; he might even leave his guns in yet a third place. If Tina had a mind to escape it would be nearly impossible to find a horse, saddle it, and ride out without waking him.

Obviously Cam was downwind from them or he wouldn't have smelled the smoke. The thing to do then was move over, circle any possible camp, move on up toward the peak, leave his horse, come back to this general vicinity, but higher, and wait for the telltale smoke of their fire in the morning.

Could be he was on a fool's errand, Cam thought, but he didn't reckon so. Even with the bounty hunters prowling around this was a big empty country. Moreover, the tracks of Chance's and Tina's led directly in this direction toward this spot. Anyway he would know more tomorrow morning.

13

After his noon meal Ben Judd went back to his office to ponder what he was going to do after Lew Kimballs' disclosure of Tina's disappearance. He had to make a show of searching for her.

As he sat in his swivel chair, feet propped up on the desk, he started organizing a posse. Just the mere idea brought a groan from him. This wasn't a country that lent itself to posses. There were few water holes and they were small and far apart, which meant they'd have to pack water for the horses if the posse was any size. It would mean wandering around the desert for days on end not knowing where to look for Tina and whoever took her. Well, he could put on a show anyway; he could lead some men to search until they ran out of water and had to return. At least nobody could say he didn't try.

His thoughts were interrupted now by the entrance of a man from the street and the sheriff looked over to the door. It was the hulking form of Crowder standing in the doorway. He'd probably come to beef about the twenty-five-dollar fine the magistrate had hung on him last night for illegal entry into Holgate's room.

Crowder moved over to him and halted and said, "I got a right to talk to your prisoners, haven't I?"

"You would if I had any," Judd said.

Crowder scowled. "Well, you've got one for sure. That's Holgate."

The sheriff slowly shook his head. "No, I freed him this morning."

Crowder looked at him in disbelief. "You what?"

"I let him go. I decided I didn't have enough to hold him on."

"Well, I'll be damned," Crowder said. "You thought you did once, didn't you?"

"I thought it over and saw I didn't have enough evidence, so I turned him loose." Under Crowder's wrathful gaze the sheriff began to get angry too. "What did you want to see him for, anyway? Just want to cuss him out?"

"You know damn well what I want to see him for. I still think he knows something we don't that he got from Mrs. Bowers. He's likely acting on that information right now, thanks to you."

The beginning of a thought came into Judd's mind and as he regarded the angry Crowder the thought developed. He reviewed it and found it made complete sense. He said then, almost idly, "How much of a crew you got, Crowder?"

Crowder looked puzzled. "Why, five men besides me. Why?"

"You wanted to talk with Mrs. Bowers, didn't you?"

"Why, hell yes. You know that."

"Well, she disappeared this morning, Crowder. If you and your men can help me track her down you can talk to her until you're hoarse."

"Disappeared from where?" Crowder asked.

The sheriff explained then that Tina had been living in the Cross house and that she had disappeared from it this morning leaving a note. The note had said she was going to Diamond K but it had lied. There was a man with her and they had disappeared. There was a good chance that this man was the bullion robber, the sheriff said.

Crowder listened carefully to all this. When the sheriff was finished talking Crowder said, "Well, they had to leave tracks, didn't they?"

"They left them. Want to look at them? First though, how do you feel about throwing in your crew as a posse?"

"Sure we'll throw in. Just so we get to talk with her after we find her."

"You a good tracker?" the sheriff asked.

Crowder replied dryly, "The army thought so. They paid me to do nothin' else for a year."

A feeling of smugness came to the sheriff then. Here was his posse already at hand, headed by an ex-army guide who had the highest motivation for finding Tina Bowers. The sheriff said then, "All right, go round up your crew. I don't know how long we'll be gone, so bring plenty of grub and water. Can you be back here in an hour?"

"Quicker than that," Crowder said and he was already headed for the door.

In less than an hour Crowder had his crew reined in in front of the sheriff's office. The sheriff, who had collected his gear at his boardinghouse, now locked the office door and mounted his horse and led the way to the Crosses'. He turned into the alley behind the Crosses' but halted the small posse short of where he had examined the tracks this morning.

Judd pointed and said, "That's where three horses were tied."

Crowder dismounted and walked over to the tracks. He got down on one knee and examined the first set and then the second. The third set was pretty much obliterated. Now he circled out into the alley and slowly walked east. Then he reversed his field and came back and picked up the tracks the horses had made where they were tied there.

As he headed back for his horse the sheriff said, "Make anything of them?"

"Why, hell yes," Crowder said. "One horse has got a crazy pair of hind shoes. You could damn near track him in the dark." He swung up. "All of you stay back and let me go ahead."

14

As false dawn came the land began to take some shape for Cam, whose horse was tied in a canyon above. He waited impatiently as full day slowly crept into being. Before it was fully here he saw the smoke billow up from a fire below him in the fairly heavy timber.

At first sight of it he did not move, waiting for more daylight to pinpoint the position of the camp. When he was able to he still did not move, for it seemed reasonable that Chance, if it was Chance's fire, would saddle the horses while Tina got their breakfast. He did not want to take the risk of Chance, going after the staked-out horses maybe far from camp, spotting his approach. He waited another twenty minutes until full daylight was here and then slowly moved afoot down the rocky slope toward the direction of the fire, which was smoking less now. It took him another twenty minutes to approach the fire and now he moved until, beginning a slow circle, he finally had a view of the camp through the *piñones*.

Below him he saw Tina squatting near the fire and beyond her the two horses and the pack mule, all ready for travel. Putting the trees between him and the camp Cam moved down the slope until, through the trees, he had a wide view of their night camp. Chance, seated on a log away from the fire, seemed to be mending a bridle, while Tina busied herself with the coffeepot and the dutch oven at the fire.

His luck was with him, Chance thought. Chance had banked on the fact that he knew where he was going, whereas anyone following him did not. He could therefore afford two fires without fear of being spotted.

Now Cam studied the camp, looking for some clue as to what Chance and Tina planned for the day. The separate blanket rolls still lay on the far side of the fire, which seemed strange to Cam. Here Chance was fooling around, maybe necessarily with mending a bridle, when he should have had all the gear stowed away, blanket rolls behind the saddles, if they were going to travel. Chance moved over now to one of the horses, put on the bridle, came back, and still paid no attention to the blanket rolls.

Cam watched them eat as they sat side by side on the windfall. Afterward, Chance had his second cup of coffee, conversed with Tina while she was still sitting on the log, and then walked over to the horses. Tina did not follow him and Cam watched as Chance untied the lead rope of one horse and the mule, mounted, and set off, leading both through the trees.

That was easy enough to understand, Cam thought. The way he read it, Chance was close to the bullion. He did not trust Tina, however, so he took her horse with him as well as the pack mule. She was stranded in camp and he would be back for her when he had picked up the gold.

Now Cam moved. He reasoned that it would be foolhardy of him to circle the camp and drop down to the wide canyon floor that Chance was traveling up toward the peak. Chance had too much at stake to risk being overconfident. If he were in Chance's place he would most certainly circle his back trail to make sure he wasn't being followed. The next move, Cam thought, was to get on the ridge, paralleling the canyon and travel its far side, checking occasionally to locate Chance. Necessarily, this was a walking job, but Chance was moving him toward his own horse so it didn't matter much.

Cam achieved the ridge, dropped over it, and gave himself fifteen minutes before coming back to the ridge under cover and checking on the valley floor. Twice he spotted Chance leading his two horses, but after another fifteen minutes walking, when he achieved the ridge he saw there had been a change below him on the canyon floor. It was pinching together and climbing, and as Cam looked up canyon, he saw something that brought a surge of excitement in him. There, just off the canyon floor, partially obscured by trees, was an old and abandoned log cabin. Above it was a tunnel into the far slope with a talus of country rock sloping down at its mouth.

Moving forward where he could get a clear view of the cabin, he bellied down and watched it. Presently, Chance rode up to the cabin, dismounted, tied his horse and Tina's to a tree in front of the cabin, and then led the mule with empty and flapping packsacks around the cabin and up the slope to the mine tunnel mouth.

Now Cam moved swiftly. Keeping trees between himself and Chance, he went down the slope, careful not to dislodge any rocks that might alarm the horses or Chance himself. When he reached the canyon floor and moved up toward the cabin Chance's horses pricked up their ears, but that was all. They did not make a sound. He stroked the nose of his dun as he passed.

Now, hugging the deserted weather-grayed cabin, Cam drew his gun and moved up to the corner. He knelt now, took off his hat, and cautiously looked around the corner of the building. The mule had been halted at the base of the short tailings slope and was tied to a low bush there. Cam could see the deep footprints in the tailings where Chance had climbed the slope and entered the tunnel.

Even as he watched he saw Chance come out of the tunnel mouth with a heavy crate which he placed on a lip of the slope and shoved with his foot. It slid down the slope and was brought up close to the mule. Chance himself disappeared into the tunnel again. In minutes he came out with a second wooden crate and slid it down the slope, afterward following it with deep lunging strides, bracing his heels in the tailings to slow his descent.

It was when he was occupied with checking himself and

watching the slope that Cam stepped out from behind the cabin and moved toward him, gun drawn.

Cam was not a dozen feet from Chance when he hit the canyon floor and looked up. There was the purest shock on his broad face as he saw Cam.

"Cross your hands on top of your head and walk toward me," Cam said flatly.

For a moment Cam could see the wild impulse in Chance's face to try for his gun. Then Chance said slowly, bitterly, "You bastard."

"Do I shoot?" Cam asked him sharply.

Slowly then Chance raised his hands, clasped them over his head, brought them down on his hat, and walked forward.

"Stay right there," Cam said and now he circled wide of Chance, coming up behind him, and lifted Chance's gun from its holster and backhanded it into the nearest brush.

"What's in those crates?" Cam asked.

"Why, the bullion that was stole."

"You stole, you mean."

"On orders."

"Whose orders?"

"Jack Carpenter's. I work for him."

"Do you now?" Cam said softly. "If you do, why'd you kill his son?"

"Billy Weaver did that. I killed Billy for it, after he killed the other guard."

"But you killed the brakeman."

"In self-defense. He was shooting at me."

Cam smiled derisively. "You work for Carpenter and he ordered you to steal his gold. Why?"

"Ever hear of insurance?"

"Maybe once. Tell me more."

"Jack had this scheme. He insured the bullion. When it was stole, he collected on it, but he still had the bullion." He pointed to the two cases.

"Why don't we go ask him?" Cam gestured with his gun.

"Load it, just like I wasn't here. But I am. Then we pick up Tina, then my horse, then we head for Carpenter."

"Suits me," Chance said evenly.

Chance asked no questions, not how Cam found him, nor how he got out of jail, for surely Tina had told him, or he'd heard it in El Cuervo. Cam watched as Chance muscled the crates into the *aparejos,* one to each side, then lashed them.

When Chance was finished, Cam waved him away from the mule and said, "You take Tina's horse, I'll take the dun. First, though, untie the mule."

"Horse stealing?" Chance asked dryly.

"Borrowing," Cam answered. "Now move."

Chance untied the mule, dropped the rope, and headed for the horses. Cam picked up the rope, followed Chance, and when Chance reached the horses he stood well away as Cam bid him. Cam holstered his gun, and, his eyes on Chance, he securely tied the lead rope of the mule to the horn of the saddle of Tina's horse. Afterward he drew his gun and waved Chance to his mount. As Chance was walking toward Tina's horse Cam said, "Keep your right hand on the cantle so I can see it."

Chance ducked under the lead rope, mounted, put his right hand on the cantle, and started down the canyon. Cam mounted and followed.

On the ride down the canyon Cam had a chance to reflect on Chance's story. Obviously, when he surprised Chance, Chance knew what he was after. Equally obviously he had rehearsed his story if anyone ever caught up with him. He had attempted a wild, magnificent bluff that he knew wouldn't work. Still, it had its plausibility. It was doubtful if Carpenter had his gold shipment insured; if that had been the case the insurance company would have supplied the guards, not Carpenter who had supplied his son. Still, in court it might make some sort of defense for Chance. Whether it was foreplanning or quick thinking on Chance's part it only underscored to Cam that Chance was both wily and dangerous. Above all, he was not yet in jail.

When they reached camp in the still cool morning Tina was sitting in the shade of a *piñon.* The blanket rolls and camp gear were in an orderly mound beside her. At sight of them Tina rose, stood utterly still for a moment as if she could not believe her eyes, then broke into a run. She was headed for Cam, not Chance.

"Hold it," Cam ordered Chance, and they both reined in, the loaded mule between them.

Tina hauled up beside Cam, smiling and crying at the same time, and she put a hand on his thigh. "Oh, Cam, you got out! You found us! I can't believe it!"

"I found something else, too," Cam said and, pointing to the mule, he added, "There's the gold, Tina."

Tina looked at the crates thrusting up from the *aparejos,* then looked at Chance who was watching this with a sour resignation, glanced back at Cam and seemingly then only noticed the drawn gun on Cam's lap.

A caution came into Tina's beautiful face. She asked Cam, "What do we do now?"

"Pick up my horse back there, take Chance and the gold back to El Cuervo, and claim the reward."

Chance was listening. He said now in a sly, thrusting tone of voice, "Who identifies me as the robber?"

He watched Tina, smiling faintly.

Tina said, "Ben talked with most of the people that were on the train that night. Somebody will recognize you."

"Will *you*?" Chance asked.

Tina looked at him a long moment, then said to Cam, "Can I talk to you alone?"

Cam knew what was coming. He nodded, lifted his glance to Chance, and said, "Get down, Chance. Move away from your horse and sit down out in the open."

"Wait a minute, Cam. Have you seen the gold?" Tina asked.

"No."

"Make him show us it's really there."

"Why wouldn't it be?"

"I want to know before I talk to you."

Cam said to Chance, "Hear that?" At Chance's nod Cam said, "Do it."

Both men dismounted. Tina and Cam, gun hanging at his side, watched Chance loosen the ropes of the pack. Chance put both hands on the nearest crate, then said, "Pretty girl, can you find that short ax in our stuff?"

Tina left Cam and went over to their gear. By the time she found the ax Chance had the oblong crate on the ground and was waiting, hands on hips.

As Tina approached Chance Cam called out, "Stop, Tina. Toss it to him. Then come here." He took a couple of steps backward and then said to Chance, "Don't get any funny notions about throwing that thing, Chance. What you do is pry off the lid, drop the ax, then back off and sit down, like I told you to."

Tina halted and now she pitched the short-handled hachet at Chance's feet, then came over to stand beside Cam.

They both were watching as Chance turned the crate over, picked up the ax, knelt, and inserted the blade horizontally in the crack between the stout cleated top and the side. With the butt of his palm, Chance drove the blade in the crack, inching it in and then prying. There was very little protest from the nails as he pried, and Cam guessed that Chance had lifted this lid before to check on the gold.

Now the nails gave up and Chance swung up the lid, using the nails on the opposite end of the crate as a hinge. This move hid from sight the gold bars and Chance's hands from Cam and Tina.

"All right, go—" Cam started to say when he heard the unmistakable sound of a pistol being cocked.

He did two things simultaneously; with his left arm he gave Tina a savage shove sideways, and his right arm swung up his gun, thumb cocking it as it rose.

Chance, still kneeling, now looking at Cam, swung up the pistol that was hidden in the crate. He made the near fatal error then of trying to rest the barrel of his pistol on the edge of the vertical lid to steady his aim for a certain kill.

In the second he was trying for a gun rest Cam shot. Only

the upper third of Chance's body was visible behind the crate lid and Cam aimed for the right shoulder and fired.

Chance was slammed over his bootheels onto his back by the impact of Cam's slug. As he was hit, his gun went off by reflex from his jolted muscles and it was pointed almost straight up in the air before it sailed out of Chance's fist and fell to the ground.

Now Cam ran for the grounded gun and kicked it between the legs of the unalarmed mule, then looked at Chance.

Already Chance had his left hand to the right shoulder, a look of pain and disbelief on his face as he lay there on his back. He began a struggle to sit up as Tina picked herself up from her sprawling fall. She brushed off her skirt and blouse and then hurried over to Cam.

He was looking at the bars of bullion in the crate and as Tina stopped beside him he shifted his glance to her.

"You knew he had a gun hidden there, didn't you?"

"I didn't! I swear it, Cam, I didn't!"

"But you asked to see the gold. Remember?"

Tina only shook her head in negation and didn't speak. Cam didn't know if he'd been cruelly correct in his accusation, but now he turned his attention to Chance who had succeeded in making it to a sitting position. His head was down and the blood from his wound was seeping through the fingers of his hand that clasped his shoulder.

"Damn coony," Cam said to him. "Have you got one stashed in the other crate?"

Without speaking Chance nodded.

"We'll leave that one nailed up." He paused. "You figured if anyone caught you he'd have a gun on you. He'd make you open the crate, like I did. If he was alone you had a chance to kill him. If there were a lot of them it didn't matter. You'd be caught anyway and you wouldn't risk a shoot-out. They wouldn't care about the guns. They had the gold. Was it like that?"

Chance nodded and said in a voice that came close to pleading, "Can you stop this blood?"

116

Cam looked at Tina. "Is there any flour in your grub?"

Tina nodded and said, "He was taking us to Mexico."

"Get it and plaster it on the holes. Find something to bandage it with."

Tina went over to their gear. Cam dragged the crate away from Chance, nailed down the lid, picked up Chance's gun, put the crate back in the *aparejo,* loaded it on the mule, lashed it, tied the mule and the horses in shade, then considered the blanket rolls and the rest of the gear. He'd leave them, for there would be no use for anything except for the water bags.

While he was thus occupied Tina had stripped off Chance's shirt. She had bathed the wound, plastered the entry and exit wounds with a thick flour paste, and then bandaged the shoulder clumsily with her spare blouse, which she had torn into strips. When this was done she helped him on with his shirt and made a crude sling out of the rest of the blouse material.

Afterward she came over to Cam at the horses, leaving Chance lying on his back, hat over face against the warming sunlight.

"I think he's got a shattered shoulder. I could feel bits of bone moving under my hand."

"What's the difference? The reward read 'Dead or Alive,'" Cam said coldly.

Tina nodded and looked up at him with a quavering smile. "We've got to talk, Cam."

"So you said. So talk."

"All right. If you take us in and turn us over to Ben the whole story will come out. My part in it too."

"Not if Chance sticks to his story." He told her then of Chance's claim that this was a phony robbery planned by Jack Carpenter to collect insurance on bullion that really wasn't stolen. Tina shook her head as he finished.

"Nobody'd believe that. I'll be called in to identify him."

"What if you can't?"

"They'll ask why he kidnapped me. There's only one answer to that. I knew he was the robber and he took me so I wouldn't identify him. They'll put it all together, now you've taken the gold from him and returned it."

Her eyes were begging him and they were beautiful, yet Cam was remembering these last few days—her evasiveness at first, her clever lying, her eventual confession of her part in the robbery, and finally of her greed.

He said with a wholly false wariness, "You're trying to tell me something. Or ask for something. What?"

"It's so simple."

"Too simple for me to see. What?"

Tina took a deep breath which lifted her bosom and came closer to him. "Cam, we've got the gold, all of it. Why take it back to Carpenter and get half of it? Turn Wes loose. We can make Mexico by midnight." She spread her arms wide in a calculated gesture of drama. "We're free. We're rich for the rest of our lives!"

Cam said quietly, "Go on."

Tina was silent a moment, amusement coming into her eyes, a knowing smile on her lips. "All right. I will. There'll be no division of spoils, no percentages for either of us." She paused, watching his face. "What I'm saying is, I'll be yours forever. You need a woman and I'm all woman. Yours. I don't ask you to marry me, but I'll be your wife and bear your children. I'll go where you go and take care of you always. I'll be your faithful woman."

Cam locked glances with her, smiling agreeably, but only just. She tried to hold that look, to passionately confirm what she had just said, but there was an opaqueness in Cam's gray eyes that was unreadable. She looked down, head bent imploringly.

"That's a suggestion, and I thank you for it. It's tempting. But if I said yes we'd both wind up in hell—you for whoring for stolen money, me for letting you do it."

Tina flushed. "Then marry me, if that's what you think. I'm free. Or would you rather see me in jail than have me?"

Cam said quietly, "Now that you've asked, yes."

Anger finally showed in Tina's face and especially in her

eyes. "What a sorry excuse for a man you are," she said contemptuously.

Cam smiled then. "Sorry or not I'm the only excuse you've got right now." He tilted his head toward the horses. "Let's hit the trail."

15

It took Crowder less than twenty minutes, or until they came to the arroyo whose banks had been caved in by the horses to halt his crew and the sheriff and dismount.

He knelt, rose, crossed the arroyo, climbed its bank, and then, satisfied, came back to the sheriff.

"We've picked up a fourth set of tracks, later ones. Could that be Holgate that you let go?"

"Likely," Judd said uncomfortably. "He's interested in Mrs. Bowers too, remember."

"How'd he know which tracks to follow?"

"Man, I'm not a mind reader. I don't know," the sheriff said shortly. He did know, but he was not about to tell Crowder the details of Holgate's escape. Most certainly these later tracks were made by Holgate's horse, for he would still be bounty hunting. And he had seen the same tracks in the alley that Crowder saw. It really didn't matter, the sheriff thought. What did matter was that his small posse was hunting Tina, as duty bid.

They made a dry camp when night came and were again on the trail at first light. It was midmorning when they came to the deserted camp of Tina and Chance.

Here, Crowder halted them short of the camp itself and ordered them to stay in this place. Then Crowder, first afoot, made his prowl of the camp.

Returning for his horse, he said to Judd, "I found some dried blood and two empty shell cases. You figure it out. I'm going to circle for tracks."

"I'll go with you," the sheriff said.

"All right. Just so you stay behind me."

On the first quarter of his circle Crowder picked up the tracks heading up canyon. When he had studied them he came back to Judd.

"Three horses up and back. Come along."

The sheriff trailed behind Crowder and they rode up the canyon to the cabin. Here, Crowder dismounted again and began to prowl. The boot tracks on the tailings were plain enough to see, and the sheriff watched as Crowder climbed up to the tunnel and disappeared in it.

When later he jogged down the slope he came up to Judd and asked, "How was that bullion packed?"

"In two wooden crates, about two-and-a-half by two by one foot. Why?"

Crowder tilted his head in the direction of the tunnel. "I think they were hid there, but they're sure as hell gone." He added bitterly, "I knew that damn woman knew."

"Why do you think they were there?"

"Well, there been plenty of dust storms since this mine closed down. There's a good inch of dust on the tunnel floor. The crates were stood on end. The prints is there. So's fresh man tracks."

The sheriff wondered what all this added up to. Blood back at the camp, two shell cases, and now some evidence that someone might have taken something resembling the bullion crates, only the latter was just a guess.

Crowder mounted and immediately lifted his horse into a trot. At the spot where they had picked up the tracks Crowder pulled his horse left to complete the circle he'd begun. He was, the sheriff guessed, trying to pick up the exit tracks from the camp.

Crowder had completed another quarter of his circle when he reined in, dismounted, examined the ground, followed something a ways, then turned, put two fingers in his mouth, and whistled shrilly. The crew appeared in less than a minute.

Crowder said to his crew, "They're headed northeast up that slope." He paused before he said, "I think they got the gold with them, so watch out for trouble."

"There won't be any trouble. According to the law that bullion is mine until I return it to Carpenter," Judd said.

Crowder looked at him with contempt and snorted. "So *you* say."

Crowder leading, the sheriff behind, they headed through the timber angling up the slope. The tracking here was easier and Crowder pushed his horse.

In twenty minutes they came to the mouth of a small canyon and here Crowder reined up again. There were signs that at least one horse had been tethered here. Its tracks joined the others and all headed up canyon.

Now the tracks swung around the peak and headed west again. When Crowder saw this he raised his arm and pumped it in the calvary signal to halt.

When his crew and the sheriff were gathered around him Crowder said, "I reckon they're headed back to El Cuervo." He took off his hat and wiped the sweat from his forehead with his shirt sleeve. "The hell with trackin' them anymore. Let's get back to town as fast as we can."

The sheriff cleared his throat. "Hold on. We're after Mrs. Bowers. You were deputized to find her."

"We'll find her," Crowder said, grinning. "She's with the gold. You can have her. We'll take the gold. All right, let's ride."

16

From Tina, Cam learned the location of Calico Flats. It lay to the northwest and now they headed for it. Chance led the way, the lead rope of the loaded mule tied to the saddle horn of his mount. Cam followed on the dun he had borrowed back, with Tina following in the rear.

The reason for Cam's choice of Calico Flats was that it had been hunted so thoroughly by the bounty hunters that it was almost a joke. They shunned it now and chose different country to search. Even if the gold had been dumped from the train there it was taken for granted by the bounty hunters that it had been moved.

When they came to the wagon road that led on to the Flats they rode abreast and now Cam observed his two companions. Chance was white-faced and in pain; he had not spoken at all, obeying Cam's orders in silence.

Tina was silent too and Cam could guess what she was thinking. Inevitably she would be deeply involved by Chance, even if Chance chose not to talk. Cam guessed that after his refusal to take her and the gold to Mexico she was trying to frame a believable lie and not having much luck at it.

Calico Flats was a long, varicolored, almost empty plain except for the railroad tracks bisecting it. Distant stock pens danced in the heat waves boiling up from this barren ground. The wagon road they were traveling paralleled the railroad and was covered by deep, powdery dust.

Cam kept watching the railroad right-of-way, knowing what

he was looking for but not finding it. And then, almost even with the stock pens, he saw what he wanted.

The arroyo that had to be bridged for the track had been thoroughly searched by the bounty hunters. The first thing they did, of course, was to set fire to piles of tumbleweed that had accumulated under the bridges. Dark splotches of gray and black ash remained.

Cam called a halt now, pulled his horse off the road and came up to the ashes under this bridge. The arroyo bottom was soft with fine sand, dented with tracks of dozens of the bounty hunters' mounts. It was as good a place as any, he thought.

He walked back to the mule, untied it, and said to both Chance and Tina, "I'm burying these crates here. If I don't find them when I come back I'll know one of you told somebody where they were."

Under the indifferent watching of Chance and Tina, Cam led the mule over to the bridge, scuffed two separate holes in the soft sand, off-loaded the crates, buried them, kicked sand and ashes over them, led the mule back and retied it to Chance's saddle horn, and brought his own horse back to the other two.

Calico Flats was a half hour's ride from town, according to Tina. Cam ordered them to leave the road and they made a half circle, coming into El Cuervo from the south in the late, hot afternoon. Cam was leading now and he moved their horses in and out among the passing ore wagons so the three-team hitches that pulled the wagons would obliterate their tracks.

Approaching the Cameo Cam saw Crowder and his crew standing on the boardwalk where they could see the sheriff's office. He supposed that in Crowder's estimation he had the status of an escaped prisoner and was fair game for capture. His hand moved toward his gun now. He knew Crowder had seen him and seen Tina too, but strangely, Crowder made no move to intercept them.

At the tie rail in front of the sheriff's office Cam ordered a halt and dismounted. Tina, her blouse blotched with the stain of perspiration, dismounted gratefully. Chance was in a daze of pain and fever and Cam had to order him to dismount and then help him to do so.

As Cam herded Chance and Tina through the break in the tie rail and under the *portal* Sheriff Ben Judd appeared in the open doorway of his office. Cam looked for the anger in his face, but there was none; he didn't even seem surprised to see them.

"So you found them, Holgate? What's Chance doing with you?"

If he can surprise me I can surprise him, Cam thought. He said to Tina, "Go up to the *Times* office and bring Amy down here, will you, Tina?"

Tina looked at him curiously, then headed up the boardwalk, and now the sheriff said sharply, "Answer my question."

"I will inside."

The sheriff stepped aside and Cam nudged Chance, who moved through the doorway. Cam looked back over his shoulder at the walk in front of the Cameo and saw Crowder and his crew mounting up. Crowder then reined his horse around and cut between two wagons, heading for this side of the street.

Stepping inside the office, Cam said, "He needs a doctor, sheriff. I think my shot broke his shoulder."

"That can wait until I find out what this is all about."

"So can you wait until Tina and Amy get here."

Chance said hoarsely, "Can I sit down?"

The sheriff gestured to the chair beside his desk and Chance moved over to it and sat down. The sheriff hadn't taken his glance off Cam. He asked now, "Why Amy?"

"I want to keep the record straight." Now Cam turned and looked out into the street. One by one Crowder's men were putting in at the tie rail in front of the office.

Abruptly, then, Amy appeared in the doorway, Tina behind her. Amy hadn't bothered to remove the paper cuffs from the sleeves of her green dress in her haste to get here.

She halted now and looked at Cam and then at Chance. "Is he the killer, Cam?"

125

"All I can say is he led me to the gold, and he tried to kill me to hold it."

"Where is the gold?" the sheriff asked.

"Between here and where I took it from him."

"Does Cam know you and Crowder and his men found the camp after they left?" Amy asked Ben.

"I don't see why it would interest him," Judd said sullenly.

"It doesn't," Cam said. "A lot of other things do, though. First, am I under arrest?"

"No," the sheriff answered and a flush came into his face. "The story is I freed you for lack of evidence."

"Yes, that would look better, wouldn't it," Cam said dryly. "Next, what do you do about Chance? Do you name him to Carpenter as one of the men that killed his son?"

"So you can collect the reward?" the sheriff gibed.

"That's why I'm here," Cam said flatly. The sheriff shifted his glance to Tina now. "Is Chance one of the robbers, Tina?"

Amy and Cam and Chance looked at her. Even after a long day's dusty ride she looked fresh and beautiful. Cam, keeping the silence he had promised himself he would, wondered what was coming.

Tina shook her head and said, "I just don't know, Ben. It's like I told you at first. I didn't pay any attention to those men."

The sheriff studied her a moment. "Then why did he kidnap you?"

"Well, he could have recognized me without me recognizing him," Tina replied reasonably. "He couldn't be sure I didn't, though, so that's why he took me away from here."

The sheriff shifted his glance to Chance and studied him. Cam noted, however, that Amy was looking searchingly at Tina. The sheriff said, "That why you took her, Chance?"

The evidence against Chance was so damning that Cam wondered what he would answer. Tina, without definitely identifying him, had given a reason for the kidnap that only drew the noose tighter around Chance's neck.

Chance straightened in his chair and winced with pain and then his glance settled on Tina. "No you don't, Pretty Girl.

126

Sheriff," he said, still watching Tina, "she was in on the robbery. She and Danny planned it. Billy and me was hired hands. We'd get a third, her and Danny two-thirds. After it was over she hacked at me for Danny's share." His laugh then was unexpected. "Sure I took her with me, so she couldn't talk. I was headed for Mexico with the gold, but not with her. Not ever. I don't hanker for a knife in my back, and she'd of put—"

Tina's eyes had rolled back, her knees buckled, and although Cam made a lunge to catch her he was too late. She slumped to the floor on her side away from him in a fainting collapse.

Amy stepped over and knelt beside her, feeling her wrist for pulse. She said the obvious. "She's fainted. Put her on the sofa while I get some water."

It was Cam who picked up Tina and carried her to the cracked leather sofa against the side wall. Amy meanwhile had gone over to the several canteens hanging by the cellblock door, opened one, and soaked her handkerchief with water. She crossed the room to Tina and sponged her forehead. As she worked gently she looked up at Cam.

"You knew all this, didn't you?" There was lingering misery in Amy's eyes, but no accusation in her voice.

The sheriff had heard her question and observed Cam's nod of assent. He came over now and halted in front of Cam.

"Why in hell didn't you tell me, the law?" he demanded angrily.

"I wasn't interested in seeing her locked up. I was after the killer and the gold."

"You withheld criminal information!"

Cam said evenly, "Yes. Lock me up."

The sheriff started to say something and then closed his mouth. He looked past Cam's shoulder at the doorway to the street. A slow smile came to his face. Cam turned his head and looked through the doorway. There was Crowder, his crew around him, waiting like so many vultures for Cam to come out.

"No," the sheriff said. "I think I'll let you go. I think there are some fellows out there that want to see you."

127

Cam had thought of nothing else since he came into this office and his mind was already made up.

Explosively, he drove his fist into the sheriff's belly. Judd's breath exploded out of him and he wrapped his arms around his stomach as he bent over, his hat sailing to the floor. Cam grabbed his blond hair then, pulled his head down. At the same time he lifted his knee into the point of Judd's jaw. There was a muffled thud and Cam let go. The sheriff fell with the slackness of a hurled sack of oats, unconscious before he hit the floor. Cam said to the startled Amy, "Go close the street door, Amy."

As she moved toward the door Cam went over to the nail where Judd hung the cellblock keys. They were just over Chance's head and as Cam took them off he said to Chance, "On your feet, fella."

He headed for the cellblock door as Chance fought to get to his feet. As he tried the door and found it unlocked he heard Amy come up behind him.

"Cam, you're in enough trouble. Why did you hit Ben? Oh, what are you doing?"

Cam swung open the cellblock door and said, "Go on in, Amy. I'll tell you later."

"Are you locking me up?" Amy asked in a startled voice.

"No. You're locking me up. Go on in."

Amy walked past him into the oven-hot cellblock. Cam waved Chance in behind her and then took a canteen from the wall hook. They both stood watching as Cam unlocked the first cell, opened the door, and gestured for Chance to enter. When he was inside, Cam moved past a bewildered Amy, unlocked a second cell, swung the door open, leaving the key in the lock, then turned and faced her.

"Amy, you've got to listen to this carefully. Believe me, it all makes sense."

"Not to me."

"It will. First, forget Ben and Tina. They'll both come around and nobody's hurt. Next I want you to lock me in this

128

cellblock. Keep the key. Remember, keep the key. Don't hang them up in the office."

"But why do I do this?"

Cam tilted his head toward the street. "Crowder and his crew are waiting for me to come out. Remember what they did to me before? Then, they only wanted to know what Tina told me. Now I know where the gold is they'll kill me to get it." He added tonelessly, "Your Ben knew that. He wanted it to happen. That's why I had to hit him to get locked in here."

Amy looked at him with a gaze that did not falter. "He's not my Ben anymore. But what does this get you, Cam. You can't stay locked in here forever."

"I won't be. Here's what you do after you leave here with the key. Go down to the feed stable and hire a rig. Drive up to the Consolidated offices. Ask for Carpenter. If he's not there make someone find him. They'll do that because you tell them this concerns his son's killer and his gold. When you find him, the first thing you tell him is that his son's killer is in jail. The next thing you tell him is that he should arm and mount a dozen of his miners and bring them here to the jail. You come with him."

"And you'll go with them?"

"Yes. Now lock me up."

He went into the cell leaving the door open. Amy started to walk away then halted and looked at him. "Is what Chance said about Tina true?"

"Yes. There's more of it and it's true too. Now hurry, Amy."

Only when he heard the cellblock door locked did he strip off his shirt against this oven heat, take a drink from the canteen, then walk over to the bars that separated his cell from Chance's. Chance was lying on his cot, eyes closed, and Cam pushed the canteen through the bars, went over to his cot and lay down. In minutes he too was sleeping.

He was awakened by a savage pounding on the cellblock door. He didn't answer and the racket ceased. Again he slept.

When he was awakened this time it was by the sound of the cellblock door being opened. The sheriff came in first, followed by Jack Carpenter, Amy, and an elderly man with a black bag who Cam assumed was a doctor.

As Cam pulled on his shirt the sheriff unlocked Chance's cell and let the doctor and Carpenter in. Then Judd came over and, hands on hips, regarded Cam, Amy beside him. Now Judd swung the cell door shut and locked it.

"I'm ready to go," Cam said mildly.

"You're not going anywhere," the sheriff said flatly. "You're right where you belong."

"Oh no he isn't," Amy said sweetly. "He belongs free."

Judd looked at her, anger in his eyes. "He attacked an officer of the law."

"Tina couldn't see the attack and I didn't see it." She paused, eyeing him steadily and then said quietly, "Or do you want me to rewrite the story of your freeing him yesterday? I can, you know."

Judd looked at her, hating her at this moment. Then, without a word, he unlocked the cell.

Carpenter was in the walkway now and Cam halted beside him. Before Cam could speak, Carpenter held out his broad hand and said, "Thanks for catching the murdering son of a bitch. I wish you'd killed him, but I'll see him hang."

They shook hands and Cam said, "You've got your men outside?"

"A dozen, like Amy told me."

"I think you'll need them. Let's go." He turned to Judd. "You coming, sheriff?"

"No," Judd said flatly. "The man I wanted is in that cell. I don't give a damn about your gold, Carpenter. You went over my head with that reward offer, so get it yourself."

"Who needs you?" Carpenter said. "Let's go, Holgate."

"We'll take your rig, Amy," Cam said, and then he added quietly, "Thanks. I'll see you when this is over."

They went through the office and out onto the boardwalk. Crowder and his crew, dismounted, stood a little to the side of the doorway, silently watching the mounted and armed guard of a dozen miners surrounding the rented rig.

Carpenter stepped off the boardwalk, headed for the buggy. He was about to step up when Cam put a hand on his arm. Carpenter halted and turned to Cam who said, pointing, "That's my horse, Carpenter. Take him and go somewhere if you want. I'll drive the rig. The reward reads that the gold's got to be delivered to Consolidated. I haven't delivered it yet."

"Go somewhere?" Carpenter echoed. "I'm going with you and my men."

"I can't stop you, but you don't have to."

"You sure as hell can't stop me," Carpenter said, and then he smiled.

"You know what this is, Carpenter. Crowder will try to pull a plain holdup. He can't claim the reward because he didn't bring in Chance. He wants all the loot and then Mexico for him."

"I reckoned you thought that or you wouldn't have asked for a dozen men." He turned and headed for Cam's horse.

The mounted guard waited for Cam to start off in the rig, then they fell in behind him. Crowder and his crew went for their horses and Cam knew Carpenter's crew would not be challenged until they were on the way back. For sure, Crowder would put a man on their tail to keep them in sight, but he would need cover that didn't exist in Calico Flats to make his attack against twice the number of his crew. Simple logic would dictate to Crowder, once he saw the barrens of the Flats, that he should hide his men under cover on either side of the road and wait for the gold to come to him.

Now Cam signaled Carpenter to him and when Carpenter came alongside the rig Cam said, "Tell your men to stay clear of my wheel tracks. I want to give Crowder a trail he can follow."

Carpenter nodded and dropped back to pass the word. His crew moved to either side of the road. Now Cam halted the rig and Carpenter again came up to him.

"You know this road to the stock pens, don't you?" At Carpenter's nod, Cam continued, "I came this road when I hit town. I figure Crowder will hide his men on either side of the

131

road where there's still cover. That's before the grade down to the Flats. He can see the stock pens from the top of the grade, can't he?"

After Carpenter reflected a moment, he nodded.

"All right," Cam went on. "He can't afford a fight on the Flats because he's outnumbered. He knows this rig can't go across country and'll have to stick to the road. Why don't we drop off three men on either side of the road at the last of the cover? After the shooting starts, our men move in on them from behind. That ought to break it up enough for us to get through."

"Good idea," Carpenter said. "I'll tell 'em."

"One more thing," Cam said. "You be one of the men we drop off."

"Go to hell," Carpenter said in a friendly voice.

"If you're dead who pays me?" Cam asked. "You signed the reward offer. You're Consolidated."

Carpenter looked at him a long moment, his face sober. "I think I know what you're trying to say. Two dead Carpenters are too many. Is that it?" Cam only nodded and Carpenter said, "Maybe you're right. All right."

Cam got the rig in motion, looked back and saw Carpenter assembling his crew. It was some minutes before they caught up with him. At the top of the grade before the mesquite began to thin out, Carpenter split the crew, and now Cam's escort was seven instead of thirteen.

They reached the arroyo beyond the stock pens without incident. The two crates were where he had buried them this morning. They were loaded into the rig and the journey back began.

The sun was heeling far over to the west and as Cam's rig climbed the grade it was in shadow. Had he guessed right about Crowder? What if Crowder's crew wasn't stationed in cover at the top of the grade, but somewhere closer to town? And what if he noted the absence of six men, smelled an ambush, and moved off to circle back and cut down on Carpenter's crew when they were together again? One thing for certain, he and his laboring horse were the prime target.

It happened just before they reached the top of the grade, just as Cam reckoned it would. There was a shot from the tall mesquite on his left. The horse of one of his guards reared and almost threw the rider. On the heel of the shot there were more shots from further back off the road and Cam knew this was Carpenter and his crew.

Now Cam seized the whip and startled his horse into a run up the last of the grade. His guards lifted their mounts into a gallop to match his speed. Suddenly, the horse of the guard on his right went down and Cam knew it had taken a slug meant for his own horse. All the guards were firing; Cam looked back and saw the downed guard on his right was forted up behind his fallen horse, shooting into the mesquite, flushing out a mounted rider who headed down the grade.

The shooting was heavy back from the road and suddenly Cam realized it was all coming from behind him. He let his horse gallop until it was wholly winded and then Cam called out to his guards, "Watch the back trail!"

He let his horse settle into a walk but did not halt him. He wanted to put as much ground between him and the still continuing fight as possible. A half mile further on Cam found a place in the road where the mesquite was so thin they had good visibility in all directions.

Cam pulled up then. The firing had stopped. His guard of miners turned their horses, faced their back trail, and swapped guesses as to their markmanship.

It was only minutes before Carpenter and the rest of the crew came into sight. One horse was carrying a double load, but there were six of them.

Carpenter gave Cam's dun to the guard who had lost his mount, climbed in beside Cam, and put his feet on his own gold. Cam put the rig in motion and let Carpenter talk. Carpenter's men had seen two men afoot run down the grade; two of his men thought they got their men. Crowder's crew apparently valued their lives more than the gold, for they had mostly panicked.

Dusk was just settling when they pulled into the shelf where the Consolidated office stood.

Carpenter stepped down and said, "Stable your horses, boys, all except the dun. Then come back to the office." Almost as an afterthought he added, "Jose, you and Fears lug those crates to the safe."

Two men dismounted and broke away from the group, and took the crates from the rig. Cam led his dun over to the tie rail and by that time Carpenter had unlocked the office and lighted two lamps. When Cam went in Carpenter was fiddling with the dial of the big walk-in safe. When he swung the door open the two miners deposited the crates inside and started to leave.

"Stick around," Carpenter told them. He went inside the safe and returned with four bottles of whiskey. Moving across the room he put three bottles on the bookkeeper's desk and said, "Help yourselves."

Retrieving the fourth bottle he walked over to his desk, beckoning Cam over. He gestured to the chair beside his desk, then sat down in his swivel chair, reached in the bottom drawer of his desk, and brought out two glasses.

Cam sat down as Carpenter poured two tall drinks. He pushed one glass toward Cam, took the other, and then a frown creased his broad forehead. "This calls for a toast, but damned if I can think of one."

Cam picked up the glass. "How about, 'Here's to more lucky days.' "

Carpenter smiled. "That'll do." They both drank and then Carpenter reached in another drawer, pulled out a big checkbook and slapped it on the desk.

At that moment the miners began to file in and Carpenter waved to them. "Drink up, boys. We've had a lucky day."

The men began to pass the bottles around, talking about the fire fight, and Carpenter turned his attention to Cam.

"There's a hundred and sixty thousand dollars' worth of gold in those two crates, Cam. Half of that is yours. How do you want it?"

"Mail me a check for seventy-two thousand. The address is Cow Springs, up north."

Carpenter smiled faintly. "You didn't learn your arithmetic good. Half of a hundred and sixty thousand is eighty thousand."

Cam nodded and he smiled too. "So make out a check for eight thousand to Mrs. Daniel Bowers. I'll take that with me."

Carpenter frowned. "What's that for?"

"For being a stupid, conniving, beautiful little liar that led me to Wes Chance. I promised her ten percent of the reward money to do it. Ask Ben Judd about it."

Carpenter shrugged. "It's your money." He opened the checkbook, picked up a pen, flipped the cap of the inkwell, dipped the pen in, and wrote out the two checks. From a slot in the desk he drew out an envelope, laid it on the desk, and said, "Address it and mail it yourself."

Cam took the pen and addressed the envelope to himself, then put his check in it and sealed it. He folded Tina's check and put it in his pocket. Afterward, they finished the drink.

Cam stood up and Carpenter did too. They faced each other, momentarily at a loss for words.

"They'll want you for the trial, won't they?" Carpenter asked. When Cam said he reckoned so, Carpenter put out his hand and said, "See you then."

They shook hands, Cam thanked him, crossed the room, said "So long" to the drinking miners, and left.

17

Cam left his dun at the feed stable to be grained, mailed his letter, and over his first meal of the day at the café next to the Cameo, he reviewed this wild day. Apparently, from the table talk among the bounty hunters at the long table, it was known that the surviving train robber had been captured. There was no news of the bullion he had hidden. That would hit town, Cam knew, when Carpenter's guards finished their whiskey and came down to town.

Done with supper, Cam went across to the sheriff's office. The office lamps were lit but the door was locked. He stood there a moment, wondering how he could reach Tina and give her the money he had promised. Amy would know, of course.

On his walk to the Cross house in the ever-present dust from the wagons he remembered the exchanges between Amy and Ben Judd today. They were purely hostile and he recalled her expression of white-lipped anger when Judd refused to help Carpenter retrieve his gold. *They're finished,* he thought, and that prospect cheered him.

The lamps were lighted in the Crosses' parlor and as he mounted the steps he could see through the front window that Amy, seated on the sofa beside a lamp, was sewing. Across the room, William Cross was reading a book.

Amy answered his knock. When she opened the door and saw him her face lit up with such a look of joy and relief that it both puzzled Cam and made him glad.

"Cam! You're back! Oh, thank the Lord. Come in."

"I'm hard to lose," Cam said with a smile. He took off his hat and stepped inside. William Cross came over to him and they shook hands.

"We were worried some, young fella."

"Not as worried as I was," Cam said.

When Cam was seated on the sofa beside Amy she said, "Tell us what happened."

Briefly Cam told them of the ambush that was ambushed itself and of Crowder's defeat, casualties unknown, and of the safe delivery of the gold at Consolidated. Outside of an interested curiosity they questioned him as trained newspaper people. Cam told them everything he and Carpenter and his crew could put together.

When he was finished William Cross asked, "Carpenter pay you?"

"His check is in the post office. I mailed it myself to myself."

William Cross stood up, said, "Well, now I can go to bed. Don't be late, Amy. You've had a hell of a day, along with Cam."

They said good night and Amy's father climbed the stairs to his bedroom above. When he was gone Cam sat down again and turned to Amy. "What happened to Tina, Amy?"

Amy was silent a long moment, watching him, and then she asked, "Are you worried about her?"

"Not any," Cam said slowly. "I have something for her. If you know where she is will you give it to her?"

"I will, but you could. She's home, under what Ben calls house arrest."

"How does that work?" Cam asked, puzzled.

"The jail is no place for a woman. Ben knows a woman in town who'll stay with her and watch her. There's a guard on the house too."

Cam considered, then reached in his shirt pocket and took out the check. He handed it to Amy, saying, "This is her share of the reward money I promised her. If you can give it to her I won't have to see her again."

Amy took the check and said, "Is that so unpleasant?"

"Yes, because the next time I see her I'll be testifying against her in court."

"What happened out there today between you two, Cam?"

"If you ever know it'll have to come from her," Cam said. Then he said, "I'll be called as a witness in Chance's trial, I reckon, so I'll be back here, Amy." He paused. "Do you ever get any time off from the newspaper?"

"However much I want. Why?"

"After the trial will you come home with me? I want to show you some country. My place. I'll have a room for you in town."

"But why, Cam?"

Cam reached out for her hand and she did not try to withdraw it. "Everyone should have choices, Amy. I could have gone to Mexico with the gold and Tina, but I didn't. You can choose between me and Ben."

"Have you looked at my hand you're holding? There's no ring there, Cam. I gave it back this afternoon." She smiled. "Yes, I'll come."